Jessica Unbound

A Novel

S.G. Kubrak

ISBN: 978-1-7375922-2-8

Also By S.G. Kubrak

The Jessica Unbound series

Jessica Unbound

Jessica Unbound: Gaia

The Dreams of a Freezing Ocean series

Dreams of a Freezing Ocean: Volume 1

Dreams of a Freezing Ocean: Volume 2 (forthcoming)

DEDICATION

For Dax and Kes.
The house is so empty without the two of you getting underfoot.
Your absence is palpable.

ACKNOWLEDGMENTS

I gratefully acknowledge the following people for their
contributions and inspiration

Editor/Proofreaders
Monica Neumark
Additional Copyediting
Carol Riggs

Cover Photo
"*Vector big data orange circular visualization*"
Image by GarryKillian on Freepik

Cover Design
Allie Shaw, DaxStudioz

Translators
Bruce Cheng and Cindy Chen,
for their help with my broken Cantonese

Talia M.X. Shaw,
for her help with my even more broken Latin.

Beta Readers
Ellison James
Libbie Kay Toler

Sensitivity Readers
Talia M.X. Shaw
Allie Shaw

Table of Contents

Chapter 1: Quantum Field Theory

It was a blustery October day as Jessica Chao ran across Washington Square Park. She took no notice of the Roman arch that led from her life as a minimum wage server at a vegan restaurant to that of a physics student. Although not the intention, it served as a bottleneck with tourists and locals passing through the space and was always difficult to maneuver. She tried hopping the chain landscaping fences on several occasions to avoid the portal, but always tripped and fell on her face.

On the concrete, however, her 5'7" frame deftly bobbed and weaved, a skill honed from two decades of growing up in the biggest city in North America. And from being perpetually late. She'd even been born late. A fact her mother politely reminded her of.

She threw a glance at her watch: 12:20. She had a full ten minutes to make her Quantum Field Theory class. She loved the subject, but this semester had been hard for her and she wanted to do her best. Being late, again, was not what she wanted.

With three minutes left, she bolted across Broadway and through the doors of the Physics Department. It was lecture and she hated coming in late; having to ask the other students what she had missed embarrassed her. Bad enough being one of two women in the class, but then being clueless as to the topic threw salt into the wound.

Jessica opened the door to the classroom and slipped into the last row as the professor stood up to start his lecture. He looked up at the clock, then at Jessica. She'd arrived precisely on time.

The professor smiled at her and started his lecture.

Her phone buzzed with a text, and she grabbed it quickly to silence it.

Did you bring me any? She read before locking the screen.

Jessica frantically flipped through the pages of her notebook to find a blank sheet. She shook her head "no", visually responding to the text. She took a deep breath to steady herself.

With lightning speed, she started taking notes. The professor had already jumped into the Klien-Gordon equation portion of the lecture. She had issues understanding how the Dirac equation related to it. Recitation didn't clarify it for her, and she hadn't met the TA to talk about it yet. Relativistic wave equations were a source of endless frustration for her, how a particle spins in multiple dimensions seemed minutia to her, and she fought her brain in its constant effort to take the problem one step at a time and not be overwhelmed with the complexity.

The badge on her phone blinked again, and the text message flashed across the screen.

Wow you stink.

Jessica's left arm shot out from her chair forcefully and slammed her closed fist into the shoulder of the person sitting next to her.

Her friend Katelyn let out the slightest of grunts as she quickly sucked in air, then bent down pretending to sneeze to cover up a laugh.

Jessica put her phone in her jacket pocket, and then looked back at the professor. Who stared, naturally, right at her. Without taking his eyes off Jessica, he spoke to Katelyn.

"Ms. Finnerty, would you care to come up to the board and finish solving for this mass, please?"

The class hushed, drawing in a shared breath that seemed to remove all the air.

"No… sir," Katelyn squeaked, "I'm sorry, I'm… not feeling well." She said sheepishly. Embarrassed at the admonishment.

"You don't have to come to class if you are ill, you know. You're an adult. Right?" He glanced back and forth between Katelyn and Jessica. Jessica immediately flushed red.

The professor held the pause at the end of the sentence for a few beats. Enough for the blood in Jessica's ears to pound painfully. He turned back to the board and added the last lines of the equation.

Jessica shook her head and took a slow breath. Katelyn dropped her head back into her book.

At 1:40, the professor put his pointer down and ended class. Before anyone could get up from their seats, and with a wave of his hand, he called Jessica and Katelyn up to the front.

Agonizingly slow, the professor put his pointer and water away, handed some papers to the TA, and then addressed the pair.

"Ladies, how many times do I have to make an example of you?"

Jessica fumed internally, feeling guilty and angry at the same time, her mouth filled with apologies.

"I'm sorry," she blurted out quickly.

Katelyn held back a smile.

"You two know you are the only women in this class, right?" He stared at them over the top of his reading glasses.

Jessica started shaking, tears welling up, and she felt the uncomfortable strangling of a lump in her throat. She didn't need to be reminded of the situation. It's the reason she ran here, why she took it so seriously, and ultimately why she pushed herself so hard.

Katelyn continued to examine anything other than the professor.

"Well?" he said expectantly.

"We're sorry," Jessica explained, choking back a sob.

"You have to be doing it better than them. It's unfair and stupid, but science is an old boys' club, especially the 'hard' sciences. You have to hold yourselves to a higher standard of behavior than…" he gestured to the empty chairs with a dismissive wave, "…some of those idiots. I don't like it, I don't agree with it, but not everyone in the world thinks in the same terms. Don't beat yourselves, okay?"

"Yes, sir," Jessica said quickly.

"Good." The professor smiled at them and took off his reading glasses. "Don't disappoint me on midterms. I'll see you next time." He grabbed his cane, the handle in the shape of a Chinese dragon, and braced himself with it, then headed out of the classroom.

The pair watched the tall form of the professor walk out of the door with the TA. He wore a leather elbow-patched brown corduroy sport coat, faded jeans, and brown wingtips. Dark brown salt-and-pepper hair, cut short. Katelyn held the stare a little longer than Jessica.

"Hey. HEY!" Jessica called to her oblivious friend. "Come on, I'm hungry. Let's get something to eat."

"Um… yeah, I know what I'm hungry for."

Jessica shook her head.

"Keep making a great impression. It will get you everywhere," she said sarcastically.

"Geez, Jessica, lighten up. He's our fathers' age."

Jessica paused for a moment and took a breath.

"Sorry… I…," Katelyn apologized.

"Yeah."

Chapter 2: Back Home

Later that afternoon, Jessica took the ferry back to her apartment in Jersey City. At eight dollars a trip, she didn't often go in for the expense — The PATH was much cheaper — but she refused to ignore the beauty of a crisp fall afternoon.

Sunlight shone down through the azure sky. The grey-green water took on a blue highlight, like little sapphires being scattered with every wave. The breeze blew hard, but not quite blowing white caps, and it made Jessica queasy if she didn't pay attention. She kept her face pointed into the breeze, and spread her feet enough to not lose balance.

To the right, the grey expanse of the Hudson River stretched up to the George Washington Bridge. Jersey City and Hoboken on the left, Manhattan on the right. Helicopters buzzed by overhead, like bees going from flower to flower. Occasionally the sunlight caught the rotors, and a brilliant blue-white flash bounced down onto the river. Under them, the nearly constant boat traffic moved to and fro: ferries, tugs, small cargo ships, and coast guard patrol boats clogged the water.

To the left, down the river and out to the sea, the Statue of Liberty held her light and faced outward toward Europe. If Jessica squinted hard enough, or if the binoculars on deck were working, she could see the statue stepping away from the broken shackles at her feet. Her stola raised in the back as she took a step both full of ease and determination. Confident in her mission to enlighten the world. Her ever-present, unblinking visage cast upon the horizon. Jessica loved how the designer imagined the statue in mid-stride; the fluidity captured in the immobile copper.

Breaking the horizon line, the rigid grey beams and arches of the Verrazzano-Narrows Bridge cut across like a knife, binding the southern Burroughs with what was once the largest span in the world. Jessica peeked under the deck and saw the vanishing point, the infinite point the ancients assumed meant the Earth stretched on forever. She forgave them their ignorance; it was just breathtaking.

In front, the dock of Paulis Hook banged against the quay. The ferry pulled in, slamming its bow against the pylons. Not worth the time or the effort to tie up the boat, the captain kept the engine at half speed. It would be loaded and underway again in three minutes. Jessica walked quickly down from the top deck, and headed off the gangway.

She walked down the three blocks and hopped on the light-rail. Six stops and a short walk brought her to her apartment

It wasn't spacious, even for the relative expanse of Jersey City, but it was home, and a few blocks from her mother, which calmed everyone down. Katelyn came and went without much warning, as was her style. At the moment, she was still in Manhattan with her boyfriend.

Jessica liked having the space to herself; she coped with life in general, and the last few years, with solitude. Her feet ached from working every day of the past week.

She drew a bath in an old enamel claw-foot tub she loved and hopped in with her textbook. After a few minutes, she gave up, put the book aside, and closed her eyes, remembering…

"Jess, I don't care how long you think it's going to take you. NYU? Couldn't you go someplace cheaper? Like Saint Peter's or State?"

"Right mom, like they have temporal mechanics at 'Harvard on the Boulevard,'" Jessica quipped. She knew full well her mother wanted her to go to college, any college, but balked at the potential cost.

Jessica turned back to her computer, her mother's tiny frame craning over her shoulder from the back. Happy, worried, sad, frustrated, and proud; all the emotions were on her face.

"I'm just worried…"

"*The Big Bad City?*" she joked, not completely pulling the punch.

"Yes, if you want to go there. It got hit so hard. We were safer over here." She crossed her arms, voice lowering.

"Mom, we got out alright. We took precautions, we did everything we could and then some. We were the only family washing groceries."

From the other room, her father's voice boomed, "I heard that!"

A wry smile turned up the right side of Jessica's lips.

"Two words: No fruit flies," he joked.

Jessica raised up three fingers and mouthed "three" to her mother. Her mother giggled. Father and daughter had the same sense of humor, and they played off each other constantly. Jessica knew it frustrated her mom —just too many inside jokes— but they were close, and it made her happy.

"Not if you hyphenate!" he called again.

Jessica rolled her eyes and turned back to the computer.

"Mom, it's N.Y.U." she said, emphasizing each initial. "It's not MIT or Columbia, but seriously."

Her mother leaned over the back of the chair, reading the screen, she brushed the straight, black hair out of her brown eyes.

"You have to let her take a chance, Ai. How will she ever learn anything without taking a risk?" her father interrupted, again from the other room.

"So, how early would your first class be?" Her mother, Ai Li asked.

"Err... I think..."

"OW!! Damnit!" her father yelled.

Jessica jerked back into consciousness. The water in the tub had gone cold, and the vanilla candle she'd lit burned out. Lifting her head from the rim of the tub, she gazed out the window of her apartment, the lights of Manhattan in the distance.

She squeezed her eyes to force the tears out, then blinked rapidly to focus. Checking the clock on the wall, she closed her right eye so she could see the time clearly.

"Dude! Are you awake?" Katelyn called from the kitchen.

"You alone?" she answered, acutely aware of her nakedness. She searched for any errant bubbles to cover herself, and came up short.

"Why would I not be? Want some wine?"

"Um, yeah." Jessica grabbed the towel from the rack and stepped up into it, wrapping the fluffy warmth around her. "I thought you were staying in the city?" she asked, grabbing her hair and twisting it up into another towel.

Katelyn came around the corner into the bathroom, holding two glasses of Merlot and extending one out to Jessica. Standing there in her pajamas she stared at Jessica, confused. "That was hours ago," she said, gesturing to the tub with her glass. "When did you get in the tub? You pulling some kind of 'Altered States' thing on me?"

Jessica took the glass and laughed at herself, "Yeah, be careful, I can run around killing animals by the river tonight." She knew she daydreamed a lot lately; fortunately no one called her on it, especially Katelyn. It wasn't her style.

"Hey, it's turning again," Katelyn said, pointing Jessica's right eye, the one that never worked right. The more tired Jessica grew, the more obvious it became.

"Well, then let's get this sucker to point all the way!" Jessica commented, raising her glass and clinking it with Katelyn's.

"Absolutely!" Katelyn replied with a wide grin.

Chapter 3: The Teacher's Assistant

Gabrielle Duncan stared over her desk at Jessica, who stared back at her ruefully. She took off her glasses and put them down on the desk, then rubbed her eyes. Her bracelet, a silver band with a single silver, polished stone, swayed back and forth.

"How many times do you want to go over this?" She asked, sitting back in her chair.

Jessica felt a pang of guilt for asking the teacher's assistant to go over the equations one more time with her. Gabrielle kept her eyes closed, and breathed softly to herself. The exhaustion showed clearly on her face.

"I just want to make sure I understand the equations properly," Jessica explained, knowing full well she understood them.

Gabrielle opened her eyes slowly as she spoke, "I know you know what you are talking about."

"I was just… worried about the other day…" Jessica tilted her head to Katelyn, who sat in the back of the classroom and pinged away on her phone.

Gabrielle grinned briefly. "You understand why we push you, right? It's more than just sexism, or racism," she started in, "it's about proving it to ourselves we can do it. If you want to confidently say you are…" her glance darted quickly about the room, verifying their privacy, "better than the others, you have to believe it first."

"So, we practice," Jessica commented, justifying her near obsession, and the reason why she had not left class, an hour after recitation ended.

"At some point though," Gabrielle explained, "you have to fly on your own. I think you're ready."

The TA smiled at her and stood; her thin but tall frame kept the straightest of lines. Jessica felt the urge to stand up, but then decided against it. She didn't want to appear to challenge her authority.

Gabrielle turned to the blackboard and started erasing the equations. Her iridescent purple blouse reflected the overhead lights and scattered orange diamond sparkles on her desk; they shifted and undulated as she rocked her arm.

"I don't think you will have any problems with mid-terms, Jess."

Jessica coughed from the chalk dust.

"It…" Jessica hesitated. "It's Jessica, Gabrielle."

The taller woman turned around and regarded Jessica as if she were speaking in a foreign tongue.

"Come again?"

"Jessica. My name." She felt herself getting hot and prayed it didn't show on her face.

Only Mom calls me Jess.

"Jessica?" She paused. "Yes, I'm sorry. You keep reminding me. I have another student… So many things I need to keep track of." She trailed off as her phone buzzed.

You'd think by now you'd remember the difference. Jessica thought, surprised by her anger.

Gabrielle texted a response, then addressed Jessica again.

"The professor needs me to help him grade some of the 101 mid-terms. I think we're ready here. You can even teach her." She gestured with her glasses at Katelyn who laughed at something on her phone.

"Thanks, Gabrielle, I appreciate your time," Jessica said as she stood up out of respect for the help.

Gabrielle stopped and looked straight at Jessica, as if she were analyzing the features on her face. For an uncomfortable few seconds, the student held her stare.

The TA smiled and walked out of the classroom, putting her cellphone to her ear as soon as she stepped away from the desk.

"Teach me what?" Katelyn asked, finally putting her phone down.

"Everything we have been going over for the exam in the last two weeks."

"Oh those," Katelyn scoffed. "Yeah, I'll get around to them eventually.

Jessica boiled at the admission. She knew Katelyn could do the equations twice as fast as her with half the effort. Things came naturally to her, she barely studied, rarely opened a book, and spent an inordinate amount of time on her phone talking to the whole planet it seemed. She exuded confidence in everything she did, and it infuriated Jessica. She never hesitated, never doubted, and on the rare occasion she wasn't one hundred percent correct, she admitted it and moved on. She broke the rules whenever it suited her. Naturally, Jessica felt a mix of admiration and resentment for her.

Yet they had been best friends since the first grade. Katelyn knew when Jessica needed someone, before she even realized it. Always defending her, always encouraging her, never testing. She regarded Katelyn as the older sister she never had. Jessica smiled despite her frustration.

"Do you need help studying? Or are you done for the day?" Katelyn asked, seeing the smile.

Jessica's temples throbbed and her stomach growled. Her double vision told her that her eye rotated toward her nose again, and she squinted to try to pull the muscle back into alignment. Laser focused on acing her exams all week, she forgot things like food, and completely ignored other lower-order demands like sleeping.

"Can we just watch a movie and hang out? You can invite what's-his-name if you want."

"Nah, he's good, I can swing by later. Vegan leftovers or are you thinking something else?"

Jessica felt the need to relax with some serious comfort food, and definitely not something she saw every day.

Only one thing could possibly fit the bill for her: "Chinese. We have some of mom's dumplings and fried rice."

Katelyn looked back at her phone, and searched for a phone number.

"You ate them all?" Jessica said with scorn. "Seriously?"

Katelyn preemptively called their favorite place to pick up replacement food on the way home. She exaggerated a wink to Jessica as she placed her order from memory.

Jessica chortled and punched her arm.

Chapter 4: Midterms

"Son of a…" Jessica stared at the screen for her Quantum Field Theory class. The grade listed there in black and white taunted her. She visibly quivered. Her hands sat on the keys, immobile save for the trembling from the tips. Tears welled up in her eyes, and her lower lip trembled.

"How could… but I STUDIED!" she exclaimed and slammed the keyboard hard, jolting Katelyn awake from the couch in the living room.

"What?" Katelyn asked, wiping the sleep from her eyes.

"My grade!" She drew out the "r" to sound like a growl.

Katelyn got up from the couch and came over to Jessica, who stood glaring at the screen. She gave Jessica a hug, feeling her fight the gesture with the rigidity of a newly installed telephone pole.

"I STUDIED!" she yelled into Katelyn's shoulder. She didn't bother hiding her frustration. Tissues appeared to materialize into Katelyn's hand and were taken instantly.

"It can't be that bad. You studied," Katelyn said reassuringly. "Let me see?"

"Yeah. FINE," Jessica exclaimed and started reading her grade report aloud. "I got an… eighty-four. You know he doesn't curve," she said, blinking furiously.

Katelyn winced at the grade.

"… and here is what… *she* said…" Jessica pointed to the screen at the comments from the TA.

> *Jessica, you know these equations inside and out. Your work proves to me you understand the dynamics. However, you aren't giving me everything I need here. Your algebra is impeccable, but nearly every time you forget to show me how the spinors relate to each other. It's like you are afraid to make an assertion on the principles. You need to show me it's more than reading the equations and doing the math. You don't experiment. There is no abstraction or application. It's as if you copied the textbook, but didn't learn to*

apply it. You're building a house with beige walls and no curtains. Take a risk, think beyond what you see.

It's not the end of the world, and I expect you to get an A on your finals. Please use this as a guide going forward. — Gabrielle Duncan

Jessica spun around abruptly and walked into the living room, threw open the door and stepped out onto the terrace. The cool air enveloped her, but she hardly acknowledged it, even though she wore a tee and shorts. She grasped the railing and planted her feet firmly down on the cold concrete floor.

"I *studied*," she whispered to herself, shaking her head. She looked out over the parking lot of the light-rail station across the street from the apartment. A train had arrived and people flooded from the exit. Some rushed to their cars, others strolled slowly, some laughed in conversation. The end of another long day, and the beginning of the weekend ahead. She snarled as her knuckles grew white from her hands clutching the railing.

A breeze blew off the Hudson River, and she felt the skin on her arms prickle into goosebumps. She threw her arms around her chest to keep herself warm. A fruitless attempt in the chilly October air.

"Hey," Katelyn called from behind her, "it's too cold. Keep warm huh?" She said, imitating Jessica's grandfather, who obsessively worried about anyone below the age of fifty catching a cold from exposure.

Jessica shook her head as she shivered.

With an audible sigh, Katelyn stepped onto the terrace and threw Jessica's coat around her. The scratchy flannel felt rough against her exposed arms.

"It's not bad," Katelyn said, glancing over at the commuters as well. "Most people would be happy with a B".

"It's… you know…" Jessica trailed off.

"Yeah, I know. Not good enough," Katelyn said with a hint of mockery.

"Don't make fun of me!" Jessica shot out. She cast her gaze up to the World Trade Center.

"I'm not. You did a great job and you should be proud of it. But it's not fair to you. You're the only person who is upset at this."

Jessica turned around and faced Katelyn, eyes puffy and turning blue.

"What did you get?" Jessica asked, her voice shaking.

"This isn't about me," Katelyn dodged.

"What?" Jessica repeated, staring fiercely into her Katelyn's eyes.

"Ninety-six."

Jessica sighed and spun back around, pulling the coat tighter.

"Babe, are you serious? Way to make me feel good about my accomplishments." She turned and walked quickly back into the living room.

Jessica tried to breathe through her frustration; she heard her father's voice in her mind.

Breathe. When you feel the tensest, is when you have to let go the most.

"I'm trying," she whispered.

"What?" Katelyn barked from the living room, a glass of wine in her hand; she was still angry, and not afraid to show it.

"I said I'm sorry," Jessica explained. "I…" she trailed off.

"You're upset, but don't take it out on me. I'm on your side, remember?"

Jessica stared at her through the open door. Katelyn's green eyes burned underneath her red hair.

Jessica sat down on the plastic chair, turning her back to the river. She cast her eyes down in supplication.

Katelyn's gaze softened and handed Jessica the glass of wine.

"Alcohol doesn't solve anything." Jessica cautioned, reminding her she drank infrequently, and she'd already had some this month.

"Nope, but it makes it easier to pretend."

Jessica waved off the drink and stepped back inside.

"Why don't you get out of your head for a bit? We need to clean up the storage downstairs, go do that."

"Are you my mom now?" Jessica rebuffed the suggestion. Her mother always gave her something to do in moments of strong emotions and Jessica thought she was just avoiding the issue. Still, standing there quivering wasn't going to help anything either.

Katelyn raised an eyebrow and held Jessica's gaze.

Jessica left the room and came back a moment later in her PSU sweatpants and NYU hoodie. Blue and white and purple and white, Katelyn called it her "Smurf outfit". It bore the distinction as her "serious comfy clothes."

"Uh oh, she's gonna get it!" Katelyn remarked, picking up her cellphone and snapping a picture.

"Yeah, those boxes won't know what hit them!" Jessica said mocking.

"Take your phone! And something to eat!"

Jessica held up the phone, stepped into her sneakers, and opened the door to the hallway. She grabbed a banana from the bowl in the kitchen.

"See you in a bit!" she said, trying to put some cheer into her voice.

"Say hi to the rats for me!"

Chapter 5: Pocket Problems

Jessica went down to the storage room in the basement of her apartment building. Although calling it a room put it generously; a four by four-foot square of chain-link fence, in a row of a dozen others. Like a dog pound for forgotten items. The storage room was filled nearly to the brim with boxes of bric-a-brac; old consumer electronics, copies of submitted papers, and bags of bags — a breeding ground for pests. She was lucky to have found nothing living there.

She dove in, moving larger boxes aside, arranging smaller ones, putting other boxes and junk in a larger box to be thrown out. Eventually. Some of the items weren't familiar at all, and she wondered if Katelyn commandeered the space to store things for her latest beau. After a while she felt she was wasting time in rearranging and not removing.

As she pushed aside an old yoga mat, the room flashed electric blue. She checked the old light fixture above her; its cold white light poured down mercilessly, giving everything in the room a pale white cast. She reached back down for the mat but grasped nothing. She whipped her head back down to make sure she indeed reached for the same thing.

The mat was gone.

She covered her right eye — the turning one — with her hand and scanned around with her left, removing all effects of double vision. It did not help.

An unbalanced box of plastic cups behind her slowly gave into gravity, and hit the concrete floor. The cups fell out and rolled away, arching gracefully around the wide limb of the stack until it hit the back wall. The blue light flashed again. The cups had disappeared too, right through the wall.

Rummaging through the same box, she found a plastic stick and pushed it through the wall. Blue light arced all around. There wasn't a feeling of pulling or pushing on the stick, but a strong vibration radiated through it.

When she pulled the end back out of the light, it appeared fine. It felt warm, but not hot. Holding it up to her face, she faintly smelled ozone.

"What the hell?" she said aloud, not believing her eyes. She knew she had studied too hard in the last few weeks, and getting an unacceptable grade had shocked her emotionally more than she liked, but she had never hallucinated before. At least not visually anyway.

She put the stick back into the wall and moved it around; a discernible shape to the "opening" emerged, about three feet tall, three feet wide, and circular.

In shock, she dropped the stick and stared at the blank wall. It shimmered, like looking through the surface of a lake; a faint blue light filled the space. She laughed nervously.

"I'm seeing things - I have to be."

Jessica took out her phone to call Katelyn, but there was no reception here in the basement.

"She's not going to believe this. She'll say I'm going crazy." Jessica held the phone up, her face filling the screen, and started recording.

"Hey, check this out! I think I'm going crazy, so I figure I'll record it for the world to see how nuts I am."

She flipped to the forward camera on the phone and picked up the stick again. With trepidation, she traced out the opening she saw before.

"Big enough to climb through," she said with a note of resignation. "Of course, it's human sized. Why not?"

For the next two minutes, Jessica silently debated the pros and cons of sticking her face through what seemed to be a small portal. One with no gravity, nor did it give off heat, yet it existed. Everything she knew about wormholes played in her head. She shouldn't be seeing this. Nothing could produce a stable wormhole without gravity in a confined space like this.

"Yeah, I'm still not convinced it's safe. I need something organic."

Jessica reached into her pocket and pulled out the banana she had grabbed before she left the apartment. She took the stick again and pulled the drawstring out of her hoodie. Placing the fruit on the stick, she wrapped the drawstring over and over it, being careful not to squish it, and allowing her to observe the peel. When she was satisfied, she held the stick back up and angled it to the opening, like roasting a marshmallow. Only it was a banana, and that was a wormhole and not a campfire.

Or she was just insane.

Sticking the food in, she slowly slid it until the entire construct was well beyond the event horizon. It felt lighter than it should be and she felt the soft vibration return. She waited for thirty seconds, then pulled it back out.

The banana, string, and stick were all unchanged. Slightly warmer, as if it had been sitting in the sun, or on her lap, but other than that, nothing was different.

She unwrapped the device, peeled the banana and cautiously took a bite. A banana, a cavendish like every other cavendish she had ever eaten.

Her anxiety screamed at her as loud as it could, commanding her to leave the area, call the police, and just get away. Who knew what was on the other side, or what could come out? How could she possibly know any of this?

Run. Run now.

"Why?" she spat into the air. "You tell me what to do all goddamned day. Every day of my life. You don't make me safer; you just hold me back."

She remembered how so many scientific breakthroughs happened by serendipity, or someone stupid enough to take the risk. Either way, it was someone who could control their fear instead of it controlling them.

She breathed deep and closed her eyes. She lifted her left leg slowly as she stuck the tip of her foot into the area. She prayed she could retract it quickly if anything hurt. She squinted and turned away, plunging her toes in.

No pain, a slight tingling and warmth.

She pulled her foot back out and examined the toes of the sneakers. They were unchanged. Putting her foot back down, she straightened her back and leaned forward.

"I'm insane."

She pushed her face through the hole and opened her eyes.

Chapter 6: Through the Portal

Before her stretched an open plain. Brown sand and rocks stretched into the distance, until they met the bright, bone-colored sky at the horizon. Above her, the sky contained one object: a brilliant, blinding white sun.

She turned around.

Expecting to see the basement wall behind her, she startled to find a metal doorframe built into the side of a large rock. She reached forward to touch it, expecting to see the blue light return from the opening she had arrived in. But nothing happened.

The metal doorframe stood eight feet tall and four feet wide. It was gray and shiny, remarkably clean. A hallway behind the frame stretched into the darkness. Etched into the lintel were three shapes which ran from left to right: a square, a circle, and a triangle.

She chuckled like someone expecting to wake up at any moment.

"I guess I'm going in."

Jessica walked in slowly, her footfalls echoing off the polished stone walls. The sun's rays did not penetrate into this passage, and the air cooled as the light faded. She drew up her hoodie and turned the corner into complete darkness.

She shuffled in the dark, hoping to not end up in a stranger situation, and slammed her toe into something hard.

The pain shot up her leg, but the eerie silence of this place forbade her to cry out. Jessica crouched down, and slowly reached out for the object. It felt cold and hard as metal. She felt around the object and mentally began to assign it shape, a rectangle, about three feet to a side.

"Camera, Jessica," she admonished herself, and took out her phone, turning on the flashlight. It glowed with a harsh white light.

With the light and her hand, Jessica searched to the left of the object and felt it connect to an even larger object made of the same material.

She felt along the edge of the large cabinet as she called it, until it ended. She brought her hand out along the space, and started moving it inward, toward where she anticipated the wall to be.

About halfway in Jessica's left pinkie began to glow softly blue, like St. Elmo's Fire before a thunderstorm. "Another one? Or is this the same one?"

She scanned around the room. The cabinet appeared to be a control panel, with countless switches. Along the back wall were five video monitors, their screens cracked and broken.

About to turn away, she noticed something in the corner of the room, where the left wall joined the back wall. She turned the phone light toward it; metal outlined the wall completely, and in the corner closest to the control panel a metal cable ran. The wall behind the metal outline shimmered and crackled, like watching an old VHS tape with bad tracking. Barely visible, the wall glowed the same soft blue.

She shook her head and her hands shook. The realization of her next move terrified her.

Resigning herself to her fate, she stepped full bodied into the frame.

She stood there, surrounded in blue light, and felt around for the edges but came up with nothing beyond the reach of her arms and feet.

She turned around and began feeling the walls until she found the opening in the same place she'd come in, and then stepped out into complete darkness.

Jessica held up the phone and viewed the display; the dark screen of the phone chilled her. She fumbled with the buttons for a moment, but it proved useless, the battery drained completely.

"Damn," she spat, and pocketed the device.

Spots danced in front of her eyes, and she felt dizzy. Quickly she sat down on the dust-covered ground and put her head between her knees.

The slowly fading blue light illuminated the room; boxes and cylindrical containers, stacked to the ceiling, lined the wall the frame previously clung to. The cabinet was similarly gone, replaced by rectangular-shaped plastic boxes.

Jessica stood up and the ceiling began to glow, a cool white light with no obvious source of power or bulb. She looked back and examined the boxes which had a simple closing mechanism, like the closure on a glove compartment. She reached out and popped it open.

"Apples?!" she said out loud, as her head began to swim.

She reached in and pulled out a few. They appeared normal, smaller than apples from her local store. She lifted one out and brought it to her nose; it smelled fine and in response her stomach growled angrily. She rubbed the apple against her hoodie, then cautiously took a bite. Ignoring the question of how fresh apples got here.

Satisfied they were safe, she inhaled the red fruit, and then reached into the box for another. She finished another one even faster, grabbed as many as she could carry, and distributed them among the four pockets of her hoodie and sweatpants.

She looked around the space. Thick dust covered the floor, no footprints, and no signs of activity, except this tunnel had a door on the end of it.

At the end of the hallway, a door made from a single piece of wood, separated her from a larger world she hoped existed. She put her hand against the door; it felt cool to the touch and a simple latch kept the door shut. She stepped back and opened the door.

White light flooded the hallway again. Sand and dust had changed to a verdant pine forest, its trees reaching up toward a pale blue sky. The white sun blazed overhead, tempered by the apparent abundance of moisture in the air. A layer of snow covered the ground between the trees and stretched into the distance.

Jessica stepped into the forest and marveled at its beauty. She reached for one of the apples yet came up empty. She reached for another and found one.

"I must have eaten more than I thought." She ate the apple and checked her remaining supply. She had four left, and carefully noted their positions.

She looked down at her footprints in the snow and then back up at a tree, "The seasons changed? Pine trees don't grow that fast. It's not seasons. I'm moving in spacetime?"

"Hello!" she yelled out of desperation, but only heard her echoed voice and the sound of the wind for a reply.

She stepped forward a few paces, looking for any signs of life, panic and exasperation overtaking her.

"Hold on, Jessica, think. THINK!"

She took a step backward and blue light flashed all around her. She fell into a wall, hitting her head, she fought to not lose consciousness as sparks danced in her eyes. When she could focus again and her head cleared, she found she was lying on the ground, staring up at a sky that was more of a brown tint than before, contrasting the blue. The gray wall of the building she'd hit rose into the sky behind her.

"Smoke?" she asked aloud, shaking her head and reaching back to check for blood. Satisfied she wasn't bleeding, she took stock of her new surroundings: a forest of buildings replaced the forest of trees.

The buildings reached up high to a common ceiling, with openings running the length of an avenue. Trash and debris were strewn about, and the buildings bore obvious signs of fires. She picked up a steel ball, rolling it in her hands. It fell to the ground in two pieces, as if cut in half with a torch.

Her stomach cramped down hard, as if she had not eaten for days, almost bringing her to her knees. She reached for her supply of apples, but to her surprise they were gone. All her pockets were empty, nothing except old tissues and lint had come with her from the apartment. She examined the spot where she had fallen, hoping to see them lying on the ground, but there were none. She licked her lips, the taste of the fruit also gone from her mouth. She felt lightheaded, and leaned against the side of the building, catching her breath.

She turned back and saw the familiar post and lintel of the doorway to the tunnel.

Whatever happened, it must have something to do with that place. It's the same every time.

Jessica walked up to the door and opened it slowly. Lights were on in the hallway and a humming sound permeated the space.

She turned the corner into the room and instantly knew her surroundings.

The control panel flashed randomly and occasionally beeped. The five monitors on the wall all currently displayed static. The frame shone as if kept in good condition. Newly added to this family of objects, a recess in the wall conspicuously appeared on the left side of the control panel. In bas relief inside the recess, the shape of a hand, twice the size of hers, reflected the white light in the room. It glowed with a hint of amber light, pulsing slowly and rhythmically. Jessica recoiled at the size of the hand, astonished at the similarity between it and her own.

Chapter 7: The Library

Jessica touched her hand to the recess and a door in the empty space on the wall slid open. It led into a large room, dominated on the long wall by a single large monitor. On the other wall stood rows and rows of shelves containing rectangular cartridges resembling books. On the short wall, opposite the door, were three alcoves, each featureless except for a single helmet-like device hanging from a cable connected to the ceiling.

The cartridges had symbols written on their sides which grew in sequence from the right side of the wall to the left, and from bottom to top. At the end near the door, several rows were empty. The backs of the shelves had small slots, ostensibly to be connected to the cartridges. The last cartridge in the last row was newer than the rest. It bore no features except for the symbols on the side, and a thin gold tab extending out from the back. Jessica turned the cartridge over, and plugged it into the next available slot.

"Well, something has to happen," she joked, but the room remained unchanged.

She moved over to the large monitor, searching for something to activate it but nothing solicited any action on the device. She turned to the alcove and inspected one of the helmets. It appeared to be fashioned to fit on a humanoid, although significantly larger than she.

Jessica took a deep breath and placed the helmet on her head and with unbearable apprehension, reached up and tugged down on the crossbar, snapping the helmet into place. Feeling a gap between the band and the back of her head — with hands shaking — she reached around the band and pressed it against her skull.

Her eyes went dark and fear gripped her body. Suddenly unable to move and no longer feeling her extremities, she felt empty, hollow, void. She screamed in her mind, and wished anyone could hear it.

Then she began to hear something: a soft hiss punctuated with pops that grew louder and clearer. The hiss faded away and the popping grew more irregular and interspersed with whistling. She saw images: ghostly images of the city full of people resembling humans but larger, blue lights flashing, people running, fire, horrible images of people and objects distorted and twisted and melting like a living Dali painting, and then the scene became calm. She realized the images were being played backward and gaining in speed. The hissing and popping turned into a buzz thar reached into a crescendo.

Then the silence and darkness of unconsciousness.

Jessica eventually came around.

She hung in the alcove, the helmet still attached to her head with her hand holding it in place. As she fumbled to release it, she felt dried blood caked around her ears and nose. She unlocked the helmet and collapsed to the floor.

As she concentrated on breathing, she heard the hiss again, only this time softer and less belligerent. Slowly it turned into words she did not understand, but they conveyed meaning-defying linguistics.

She squeezed her eyes tight as she tried to discern anything useable from the chaos. Equations floated in her mind: numbers, matrices, derivations, everything she had failed to see the complexity of in her exam. Energy and particles spinning together, complementary and contrasting, splitting into two, four, eight, sixteen, stretching to infinity then coalescing into one.

Opening her eyes slowly, she saw glimpses of the control panel, instinctual information on their operation flashed in her mind. The more she grabbed for it, the more it stayed just beyond her reach.

Breathe.

Jessica took a slow, deliberate breath. Bringing the air in through her nose, and out of pursed lips. She repeated it twice, and felt her mind calming, becoming clearer.

Quickly she walked out of the library, knowing what she had to do. She headed to the control panel and studied it, matching controls to the images she still saw in her head.

"Okay, let's do this," she said, willing her hands to stop shaking.

She threw switches on the panel, not thinking, but reacting. She knew if they still functioned, she could open the gate to bring her home. She hoped. She really had no idea if the data was accurate.

Who knew if it still worked properly? Or even if she would ever come out on the other side.

She remembered the apples and how they disappeared.

"Something happened. Something not right." She laughed at the absurdity of it.

"I'm either on some strange planet with malfunctioning wormhole gates..." she flicked a few more switches and grinned at the sound of electronics powering up, "or I'm on the floor of the storage room after eating rat poison."

"Vibrations," she said to herself as she rapidly flicked switches, styled in a language she didn't understand. "I'm vibrating at the wrong rate. I'm in a different universe."

She realized how absurd that sounded too, and deep in her mind her anxiety screamed as loud as it could, but given all of her recent experiences, this hypothesis fit the facts.

Or I'm just deluded, Occam's razor reminded her.

More switches thrown, and the frame came to life. It hummed and glowed; the space inside filled with the blue light that brought her here, and which would hopefully take her back.

While finishing the activation sequence she began to doubt herself. The information started slipping in her mind, like picking up dry sand on the beach. It took more and more of her concentration to recall the images guiding her on which buttons to push. A full five minutes rushed by as she scanned the now active monitors for the opened gates and their coordinates, if any still existed at all.

Then she found what she thought would be home — the top of a list of glowing squiggles and lines — and punched them into the console. She had the fleeting thought by doing this the chaos she saw in her mind might return. But if she didn't, there would be no way to get home. She had to take the risk.

She pressed the commit command, and the frame's light burst into double intensity. The gate yawned open, like the mouth of a hungry tiger.

Jessica took one last look around, breathed deeply, and walked through.

Chapter 8: Bellerophon

Jessica opened her eyes slowly, feeling like they were filled with glue; they struggled to obey. Her stomach continued its incessant growl. Painfully so. Eventually, she focused on the ceiling above her and scanned around trying to remember her actions to this point.

At first it appeared as if nothing had changed. On further inspection, there were obvious differences. All the machinery worked here, the cabinet, the frame, and the monitors. She squinted up at the five of them, which were displaying video now instead of static. With her rapidly clearing eyes, she could see the city as it stood before, as she recalled from the images in her mind: air-cars, lighted buildings, the clear blue sky, even… people?

It wasn't a distant recording of a long-dead civilization, or one in chaos; they were here, now, and as she focused on the larger of the five monitors, it showed one person walking toward her.

Her head snapped in the direction of the hallway, one she had been in so many times, now with a door about to open. Quickly she threw herself into the corner between the frame and the control panel, making herself as small as she possibly could. Her heart pounded in her chest - she knew anyone could hear it, had to hear it. With the portal inactive, she knew she could not escape this time.

The door snapped open instantly, far quicker than anything she had experienced before. The sounds and scenes of the outside flooded into the hallway; the tall figure stepped in, silhouetted against the street, casting a long shadow.

Jessica stopped breathing instinctively, and her body shuddered.

The door slid closed as quickly, and the room plunged back into darkness; the lights from the monitors and control panels glowed on, casting the room in eerie blue shadows.

The figure stepped into the middle of the room and stopped, standing still in the darkness. After a moment, it spoke aloud, a guttural half-bark, half-growl. Unlike anything she had ever heard before, although it wasn't loud, it possessed a commanding tone.

She had to breathe and chanced a shallow breath.

Almost instantly, the figure spoke again, in the same tones.

Heart pounding and head swimming, Jessica desperately tried to stay conscious.

The figure shifted and the lights exploded into the room. Its hand shot out and pressed a contact on the wall, plunging it back into darkness.

The same phrase this time, softer.

From what she could see in that glaring moment, the figure appeared vaguely human, tall with a massive frame. Green eyes with no sclera, bald head, and grey skin. She couldn't tell if there were ears. It wore a grey suit of sorts, form fitting, but exceedingly bulky in places. If it had a gender, she couldn't guess it.

She could hear it breathing in long, slow breaths — a complete contrast to her shallow staccato.

Her stomach growled like a caged animal, and the pain rampaged her body, her eyes unfocused.

It sounded like the figure found this situation amusing. It let out several barks, quick and deep.

It spoke again, relaxed, with completely different words.

With a thud, it sat down on the floor in front of her. It started speaking again, straining to form words.

"…kkkrra…b-baaaahhh," it said.

Jessica tilted her head, she had no idea what it said, but it sounded like a language she had heard before.

"…annn…row…po…" It waited.

She realized what it was trying to do, but terror kept her from speaking.

"…j — ja hhnnnn…" it quickly breathed in, "…jhan."

She understood a word. The word for "person" in Cantonese. Out of instinct and twenty-two years of repeating, badly, to her grandfather, she responded automatically, "Dueah." Terror tore through her body; she'd given herself away completely.

It drew an even deeper breath and shifted on the floor, grunting softly.

A light turned on below its face, its pale, amber hues reflecting off its green eyes. It smiled and lifted a hand to its face, where it pressed unseen buttons on its forearm. An amber, translucent square leapt into the air — projected from its wrist — and spoke in the same guttural language to the alien. Soft measured tones, indeterminate of gender.

In a series of grunts, Jessica again heard "jhan," then the square disappeared.

To her complete astonishment the figure began speaking Cantonese.

"Ngoh bat wuih seung hoih neih dik. Neih han on chyuhn. Neih ngoh liuh ma?"

Its harsh vocalizations were still being spoken but were now translated to Cantonese played from the amber square. The large alien smiled, pleased with itself.

Jessica didn't speak it well. Born in Jersey City, she knew more Spanish than any of her "native" tongues. It was something her mother always regretted not being more insistent upon after hours of discussions of "heritage" and "birthright" and innumerable false starts. Her father spoke more than she did. She desperately wished she'd taken it more seriously as a child, and even her fairly respectable knowledge of American Sign Language was now useless.

"Ngoh mm jidou," she said, after thinking of "I don't understand" in ten other languages. Although she did recognize the last sentence, "Are you hungry?" uttered to her hundreds of times by her grandparents; she didn't want to base an entire conversation around food, though.

It sat back and regarded her quizzically.

Flipping its wrist back up and showing the square again, it started speaking in its language. Then it held its wrist closer to Jessica, illuminating her face in the darkness. The square started speaking to her in languages she could tell were from Earth, but none she understood. She could hear Swahili, Cantonese again, a Middle Eastern language she couldn't understand, then *hominem*.

"Person," she said to the square, recognizing Latin.

The square floated, quiescent for a moment, then spoke with the large alien looking on, "Ego flamma non ardebit in te. Quae te dolor? Esurisne? An de Terra?"

She recognized Terra, the Latinized name for Earth. From its speech she could glean "I won't hurt you. What is your pain? Are you from Terra?" Her brain screamed, Terra? How could they know? Jessica resisted responding in Spanish, another road she couldn't drive all the way down.

"I am Terran. I do not speak Latin. Do you speak English?" She decided to respond in the only language she truly understood. She spoke slowly, careful to not use contractions or idiom.

Frustrated, the alien pulled its hand away and stood up quickly. Jessica flinched in surprise and pulled her knees closer. It pressed the contact and the lights flooded the room.

As figure and the glowing square began to have a conversation, it went into the library and pulled cartridges off the walls. Jessica stood up and timidly followed.

This version of the library dwarfed the one she just left, with rows and rows of shelves full of cartridges. The main screen, currently on, showed the sky outside, air-cars occasionally streaking across the view. The three alcoves each had a helmet like she had used before. Everything gleamed spotlessly, with warm wooden tones with grains utterly alien to her.

The tall alien went behind one of the rows, and left Jessica standing there by herself. She felt unsure of what to do, but apparently it trusted her enough to leave her unsupervised. She examined the room, trying to draw in as much as she could. She needed this… person to help her; she was totally at its mercy.

It came back a moment later, smiling and holding up a cartridge that appeared old and well-worn. After walking over to the wall next to the door, it pressed another contact. A control panel and slot emerged on a simple track. The tall alien pushed the cartridge in, and then pressed another contact.

The main screen changed to a series of squiggles and lines Jessica recognized as the written language of this planet. It scrolled line after line of text and then stopped.

The square spoke to her again in Latin, "Hoc gerunt. Eam docebit vos loqui."

Jessica squinted her eyes, desperately translating and coming up short. "Wear… speak?" She shook her head and raised her shoulders.

"Scientia," it said again, slowly.

"Science… docebit…oh, teach! You want me to put on the helmet again so you can teach me how to speak?" she said, pointing to the helmets in the alcove, then gestured to her head.

The alien raised its hand and pointed to the alcoves containing the helmets.

Trepidation froze her; the last time she wore one of those she lost consciousness for hours and nearly lost her mind.

The square repeated, "Ego flamma non ardebit in te." Again, promising to not hurt her.

Suddenly, her stomach knotted hard, and she bent over, clutching in pain desperately trying to breathe. Fighting to stand the pain became excruciating, and she dropped to the floor.

The square quickly spoke in the alien tongue, and the figure hurried back into the control room, calling back in its soothing voice. "Ego auxiliatus sum."

"Please… h-help," Jessica croaked out, curled in pain.

A moment later the alien crouched down by her side, softly growling, sounding more like a purr. Blinded by the pain, she felt the alien pull the hoodie down from the back of her neck, and then felt its enormous hand hold her spine delicately. In the other hand it held a small grey square, one inch on a side, and moved it toward her neck. She had no choice but to trust it, and she willed herself to relax as much as possible. A spot of cold made her twitch reflexively, and then as fast as the pain had arrived, it disappeared.

Jessica sat up slowly, still immensely hungry, but no longer in pain. She looked over to the alien and smiled, reaching back to her neck.

"Non tangere," the square said softly.

The hulking alien helped her to her feet, and pointed back to the helmets silently waiting in the alcove.

"Well, you obviously don't want me dead, or to imprison me… yet," she said as she stepped into the alcove and pulled the helmet down, moving fast before her anxiety caught up with her.

"Here goes nothing." She pressed the band to her forehead.

Her eyes went dark. Unable to move, she could no longer feel her extremities or anything in her body. As before, she felt empty, hollow, and void; this time she allowed herself to relax.

"Cookie…," she heard in her own voice in her mind. She instantly knew it, her first word. Or at least what her parents told her it was.

An image of her mother, "mah-ma."

Her father, "bah-ba."

Picture books from her childhood. Small words. Bigger words. Chapter books. Textbooks. Mandarin, Spanish, Latin, Cantonese, English, Polish, ASL. It all jumbled in her mind, increasing in speed. This time it became intoxicating. Now this planet and their culture. Words she saw before and could recognize: barking, grunting, trilling, beeping, clicking, and popping. It slowed down in her mind and calm slowly replaced excitement. One final word, almost like a dictionary reference, sat in her head, "Bellerophon," with the text of the alien language sitting beside.

She opened her eyes. The alien smiled down at her; it spoke in its guttural tones and growls, but she understood it clearly.

"I'm fine. Thank you. I understand."

Chapter 9: Orvalus

The hulking alien stared down at Jessica's small frame and smiled. The translucent amber square floating above its wrist spoke.

"You understand me now, Terran?" it said in perfect English.

"I do!" Jessica beamed. "You learned English when I was learning… Standard?" She paused to search her memory for the proper word to describe their language.

"Obviously. We could have stayed with Latin, though. I find it much more descriptive. Germanic languages are so harsh, like my friend here."

Hand quickly to her face, Jessica tried to suppress a giggle. She glanced at the dark green eyes of the alien, but it did not respond.

"It doesn't speak it yet?"

"My companion, Orvalus, does not yet know how to speak English. He will step into The Teacher and learn as you did."

The square switched to Standard and spoke briefly to the tall alien.

At the hearing of his name, Orvalus stood more erect and placed his hand over the center of his chest, bowing slightly. Jessica responded and respectfully stepped back.

In a quick two strides, Orvalus cleared the span of the room and stepped into the leftmost arch. With the calm of someone who had been through the process hundreds of times, he grabbed the helmet and snapped it onto his head. In a second his eyes closed and his body twitched gently.

"How…?" Jessica asked.

"Brainwave manipulation."

The voice of the square permeated the room, coming from everywhere and nowhere.

"The Teacher manipulates the brainwaves of the student and in so doing, alters its structure and neurotransmitters. Your Terran brain is more primitive and transference is more difficult and time consuming. However, it afforded the ability to learn many things about you."

Jessica felt a slight twinge of offense as Orvalus stepped back out of the arch, releasing the helmet to hang in the space.

"Hello, Jessica," he said when he stepped out and spoke in a deep, resonant baritone. "I can understand you now. We can speak both languages now. There should be... no lapse in communication."

"I'm the only version of English you have here? What about all the Latin and Cantonese?" She spoke into the air, hoping the square would respond.

It did, this time from Orvalus's wrist.

"The gate to Terra has not been open in some time. We have not had any visitors from your dimension since the Time of the Trials. None of them spoke English."

"How long ago? Wait... dimension? So, I am in another dimension?"

"That is correct, Terran. You are in another reality to your own. The portal network can traverse spacetime as well as different dimensions. Parallel existences, to put it in a phrase your culture can understand."

Jessica accepted the fact quickly. So easily she surprised herself. If this were in fact a delusion, she was obliged to follow it to its conclusion. If this were real, then the same properties of wormholes in spacetime could conceivably apply to other dimensions. She moved on quickly from the mental gymnastics and focused on the matter at hand.

The square switched back to the room.

"It has been one hundred fifty-seven standard years since the last Terran visit. Eighteen-hundred years on Terra."

Ever the student of history and centers of learning, she deftly reached a conclusion. "The gate was in Rome?"

Orvalus stepped back, surprised. The square waited a moment before speaking. "Very perceptive. You surprise me, Terran."

"The gates link into a multiverse, with time and space as variables?"

Orvalus chuckled as he walked into the main room with the frame. "You know much small one. Careful Dee, she is... smarter than you think," he called back.

"It has been quite a while since I have encountered one from her dimension. Apparently, they have evolved since then," it paused, "although not as much as I had hoped."

The disdain trickled in, and Jessica again ignored it. But did not forget the tone.

"This universe vibrates at what frequency?" she asked.

Orvalus roared with laughter and came back in from the control room, a large plate of apples and dates in his massive hand.

"It…" Dee paused, then continued, "vibrates at twenty-three centimeters."

Orvalus pressed another contact, and a table and two seats grew up from the floor. Jessica jumped reflexively, then eyed the food hungrily.

"Is this safe?" she asked, recalling all the pain she had been in each time she ate something.

"Yes, perfectly." Orvalus sat down and offered her the plate, "The patch we put on your neck… speeds you up to our frequency. Do not remove it, or jostle it unnecessarily. If it breaks or detaches, you will eventually drop out and… disintegrate."

The searing pain flashed back into her mind, and she became acutely aware of the patch lying quietly on her neck. Jessica shook her head, "This is crazy. How long have you, you know, visited us?"

"I have guarded the Terran gate for the last…" He tried to do the calculations in his head.

"One hundred ten years," Dee commented without prompting.

Her mouth watering and stomach growling, Jessica sat down at the table — the chair molded to her body as she did — and grabbed an apple. Biting into it, she tasted the sweetest one she had ever eaten, although she could not identify the variety.

Orvalus continued, "I have not been here long; however, we have… visited Terra for many thousands of your years, dating back into your antiquity. You are the only other species of sentient beings we have encountered."

"You brought apples back? As trade for something? A kind of exchange?"

"I believe the word would be… 'sacrifice.'"

Jessica choked slightly.

"Your simple society thought we were gods. You could not comprehend visitors from another dimension, as such we perpetrated the cover in order not to interfere with your culture. We learned a great deal about you and how your society functioned," Dee explained.

Jessica swallowed a date she had barely chewed and drank the water Orvalus had gotten for her.

"We?" she asked turning to Orvalus and then up into the air. Dee responded to her.

"Yes, sentient AI enabled our culture to be able to create the gates. Without us, the computations would have been impossible to derive. We have lived together for many thousands of years."

"Created by…?" she implored Orvalus. "I'm sorry, I never got the name for your civilization."

"There is none, we go by 'The People' for sentient beings, and 'The Hegemony' for the civilization at large. We created the AI and together we created the society you see before you. We no longer make the… distinction between organic and synthetic life." Again, Orvalus showed visible pride in his society's accomplishments.

"Dee…?" Jessica asked. She had more questions about them than they had of her at this point and showed no timidity in asking.

"D417a is my full designation."

"Heh, Dihedral four. Square." Jessica recalled her geometry.

"Yes, I rather enjoyed the borrow from the Greek."

"You were on Earth?"

"Yes, I visited Terra. We do not use the Germanic name for your world."

"Visigoths." Jessica nodded her head, biting into another apple.

"Barbarians. So uncivilized."

"How did you… how could you…?" She studied the rotating translucent square floating above Orvalus's wrist.

"There are other forms I can assume. It is easy to disguise myself on your primitive world."

Jessica jumped in quickly, "Can we take a break with all the Terran bashing? That was over a thousand years ago, and you've no idea where we are now."

A palpable silence filled the room, she quivered with anger at having been insulted one too many times.

Dee spoke, "In learning what your mind told of us of your world, you have not advanced ethically as far as you have technologically. You are still primitive in your understanding of the universe and your place in it. However, I understand how this might hurt your ego, and it does not lead you on the path toward enlightenment if you are mired in anger and resentment. I will refrain from using such language in the future. Forgive me."

Taken aback by the quick turnaround, and not completely convinced of Dee's sincerity, Jessica nodded in agreement. She would remember and hold him to his oath.

Orvalus chimed in, attempting to break the tension. "We have not talked about the… obvious issue here, my friend." He regarded Jessica after swallowing a date without chewing it, "What were you doing in the transit system? How did you get here? What have you seen?"

The grad student swallowed and acquiesced to the question; the time had come for her to respond. "A portal opened up in my apartment in the basement. I have no idea why. I study physics on Ear… Terra, and I could not ignore it." She emphasized the "not." "Come to think of it, it was pretty stupid to pop my head into a strange glowy thingy."

Orvalus chortled.

"So, I bounced around a bit trying to figure it out. But I always ended up here, on Bellerophon. I used the Teacher on another … version?" her voice up-ticked, not sure if she used the term appropriately, "And I learned about the Trials, I'm presuming, and the coordinates of Ear…" she sighed, "Terra. But it didn't work. I thought I had it but I'm still here."

Dee chimed in, "Because KT has blocked all access to Terra, in any time period, or parallel dimension."

Jessica looked at Orvalus, and before she could even ask the question, he responded to her.

"KT controls all of the gates The People use. It was created to… keep us safe, networking the stable planets and dimensions. More than a dispatcher, but less than a despot."

A chill ran down Jessica's spine at the word "despot." She'd heard, and seen, too many examples of control structures intended to protect people and then end up being their absolute ruler; also the relative ease with which Orvalus threw out the term unnerved her.

"Why did it block Terra? Is it a firewall? Which way is the block? Outgoing or incoming?"

"Because of The Trials, the Terran gate was unstable. Dee could probably explain the physics of the situation better than I. To spare the fate of the multiverse, all the unstable gates, and all of the ones not controlled by The Hegemony were… shut down. Travel toward an unstable gate directs the traffic back to the point of origin."

"Which is why I couldn't get away from Bellerophon once I'd arrived?"

"Yes, KT directs it all back to the next stable location based on vibrational frequency. Or purges it from the system."

Jessica remembered the searing pain from the last time she collapsed. Sensing this, Orvalus responded.

"Yes, small one, another jump and you would have been… erased from existence." A reverent tone filled his deep voice.

"I don't get it - how did I get into the system at all? How are the gates from the Trials versions of Bellerophon still working? I bounced in more than one dimension, didn't I?"

"I do not know. The Terran gate and its instability within spacetime may be the cause. KT has its… reasons. Did your world conduct experiments with hyperspace? Neutrinos perhaps?"

Jessica tried to remember, searching for something that could be a key to the mystery. But as a grad student, she wasn't privy to any major projects, and certainly not any secret ones.

"I have no idea; my world is scattered right now. It's pretty unstable."

Orvalus nodded and although she couldn't hear it, she figured Dee had an unvoiced opinion.

"And you work for KT, a gatekeeper?"

Orvalus sat up with pride, again placing his hand on his chest and bowed.

"I have been Gatekeeper of the Terran Gate of Bellerophon for one hundred ten of your years. But KT is not who I work for." He pointed to the square floating quiescently above his wrist.

Jessica quickly tried to get a better feel of their relationship. Something didn't make sense to her, but she decided not to press it for fear of being too nosy. She had no idea what could set them off. "So, where do we go from here?"

"That," Orvalus intoned, "is a *very* good question."

Chapter 10: D417a

"Protocol dictates I am to report any deviation of gate performance to KT without delay," Dee stated flatly.

Orvalus pointed to his wrist in agreement.

"I would like to see you returned to your home, Terran," Dee continued, "but I am afraid if we notify KT, it might take harsher measures and attempt to purge you from the system. Our directive of no harm to The People does not cover animal forms of life." It paused, sensing the error. "Or to denizens from other dimensions as you know."

"Perhaps we can find a way to convince it, and allow her to return?" Orvalus asked.

Jessica sat back in the chair, as it reshaped itself to support her repose.

"KT cannot be 'convinced' of anything. Its logic is infallible," Dee retorted quickly.

"Then, logically…" Orvalus said, "we find a way to elevate her status to 'not-animal' and return Jessica back home, lest she suffer in captivity."

Jessica nodded emphatically. The pair paused, waiting for Dee to speak.

"We will need to bring more to the discussion than the desire to prove the Terran is not an animal. KT will want assurances from more than the three of us. I do not have the capacity to debate it on my own."

"Administrator Dux," Orvalus said quickly. "She is always searching for a way to… increase her standing in the city. This would be advantageous for her."

"The administrator rarely takes visitors; we will need persuasion to see her at all," Dee said.

"I know someone who can help. We can do this."

Jessica smiled at the large alien, or rather she was the alien at this point. He regarded her with a broad smile.

"Well," Orvalus said, standing up from the table, the chair melting back into the floor. "We need to leave this place. I am tired of waiting. Is that… 'Okay' with you, Dee?" He used the English phrase with trepidation. Jessica smiled.

"It would be beneficial to see how the Terran interacts in our culture. This might facilitate her enlightenment."

"Good idea!" Orvalus said, walking toward the hallway and the exit door.

"Wait!" Jessica called.

"Yes, Jessica?" Orvalus turned and smiled at her quizzically.

She gestured to herself, pantomiming her appearance with an awkward smile.

"You are the size of a child, no one will notice you," he said.

Frustrated, Jessica pointed specifically at her face. Tan skin, brown eyes, dark brown wavy hair with green highlights. The opposite of her hulking companion. "I don't look like you."

He stopped and pondered the situation, seeing how different she appeared. "I will return." He smiled, then headed out of the door. The bright white sunshine poured into the hallway for a brief moment. In a short time, Jessica noticed children were, in fact, her height and even close to her build. Aside from the skin and eyes, they could easily pass for human. The adults, however, could all be the starters for a professional basketball team. Many were even taller than Orvalus.

She slumped back down into the chair and ate the last date. "I have no idea what to do here," she said.

"Is there something else you require, Terran?" Dee's voice filled the room. Jessica sat upright.

"I thought you were with Orvalus?" she asked.

"I am. I am also here with you. I am not currently bound in a physical form, and therefore can be in many places at once. It does not task my memory to do so. Rarely does anything do that anymore."

"Why?" she asked and immediately regretted the rudeness of the question. Dee answered without missing a beat.

"I was brought online to study Terran culture specifically. Since the gate's closure, I have had little to do other than review old data, and converse with Orvalus of course."

"Have you always been partnered?"

With a hint of indignation, it responded, "I am not Orvalus's partner. I am his superior. He has been assigned here to assist me. Although I could accomplish all of my tasks without his assistance, he is kept on in the event of dynamic situations that I cannot physically deal with."

"He's your 'muscle,'" she said.

"Muscle? Yes, you could say he is the arms I need when I do not have my arms."

"You have arms? Where are they?"

"My workshop on the other side of the city. My exoskeleton and ancillary parts are stored there. I do not need them mind you, and I find for the most part they are an impediment to me. However, if it becomes necessary to take physical action, and I am without Orvalus's assistance I can transfer myself there. I have never needed to do so, and for that I am thankful. I find having a physical form extremely limiting and I do not understand how you tolerate such an existence."

"It's the way we are."

"Yes." It paused. "Have you ever considered transferring your mind to a robotic form? Or forgoing a body completely and having unlimited freedom like I do?"

"You mean like an android?" she asked, shocked at the idea.

"Not like an android; I am a *de novo* AI, not a mere automaton. We call uploaded biologicals *emulant AI,* as in emulated personalities. They are minds housed in android bodies. It would avail you of so many things and free you from the limitations of a physical form, including death."

Jessica immediately thought of her father and sighed as she attempted to fight off the emotion. They could have uploaded him before… "Honestly I haven't considered something like that. I like my body at the moment," she said and tried to change the subject quickly. "There aren't any Terrans in this dimension?"

"No, there are not. Your planet does not even exist, although your star still shines. The People are the only sentient species besides yours that we have encountered in the forty-six stable dimensions and fifteen thousand habitable worlds."

"I'm not even sure which planet I'm on."

"Bellerophon, using the Terran name, is the fifth planet in orbit of the star MX6481, Tain Jin si."

Jessica squinted, trying to translate. "Deneb?"

"Yes, using the Arabic name, you are correct, Terran." Jessica could hear the surprise this time.

"So, I'm what, twenty-six hundred light years from home?"

"Two thousand, six hundred and sixteen light years to be precise. In a different dimension, do not forget."

How could I? You keep reminding me.

Jessica stood, waiting for Orvalus's return. She felt ill at ease speaking to an AI that had shown time and again its disdain for her. She switched the questioning back to her.

"What happened during The Trials? What went wrong?"

The AI was silent for a moment, then spoke. "An instability in the universe caused some of the gates to collapse into microscopic wormholes. They are unstable and do not transmit all of their information cleanly, resulting in errors. The errors self-replicate, spreading the instability exponentially."

Jessica recalled the Daliesque images in her mind, as well as the screaming. Dee continued.

"The appearance of so many errors de-stabilized spacetime and began tearing holes in the continuum itself. Frightened, the citizens fled in any way they could. A few chose to hide in the more stable pocket dimensions, and others hid on other planets and then powered down the gates to prevent more disruption. Other dimensions collapsed with no warning. Finally, some were intentionally purged to preserve the integrity of the remaining connected dimensions. It is a tragedy to science."

Jessica tried to piece what she knew together in her mind. She thought of the infinite number of collapsed universes. The untold loss of life dumbfounded her. "Will my dimension be purged?"

"I do not know, Terran. Only KT understands the permutations of that reality. That is its sole function."

Now I am become Death, the destroyer of worlds.

"Your heart rate and breathing have elevated. Are you unwell?"

Jessica shook. "I didn't ask to come here; I didn't want to open the gate or portals or whatever you call them. This isn't my fault."

"Gates are controlled site-to-site wormholes," it corrected her. "Portals open without focus and cannot be controlled or are the result of a gate establishing a new connection. Indeed, this is not your fault, Terran. However, this is now your responsibility. Getting things 'back to normal,'" it used the idiom it learned from Jessica's download, "should prove interesting."

The door to the city opened up again, and Orvalus entered, smiling.

"I have found the solution; we will disguise you as… my niece." He beamed, and threw a pile of hideous clothing on the table.

Chapter 11: Stepping Out

Jessica stared blankly at the lump of cloth; it resembled an old tarp someone pulled from the trash after a sporting event. Dirt and oil stained what she took to be the front of a jumpsuit. The boots, caked in mud and plant debris, dripped with water. The clothes reeked of what she could surmise to be body odor. The most agreeable aspect of the whole outfit was the steel grey color of the one piece; it had a sort of angsty appeal to it, though she would have preferred darker. Her stomach churned as Orvalus lifted it and a bug crawled out and scurried across the floor.

"I'm not wearing that," she said flatly, shaking her head in the negative.

Orvalus scanned the suit and turned it around in his massive hands. "What is wrong with it?" he asked, unsure of the cause of her refusal.

"It looks like you pulled it out of the garbage, or you mugged someone to get it."

"Mugged?" Orvalus asked, unfamiliar with the term.

"Removed the article from a person by use of force," Dee chimed in from the room.

"Ah," Orvalus responded. "I did not … *mugged* anyone. I traded it with a short gardener working outside."

"Traded what for it?" Jessica said, hesitantly holding the suit by two fingers on an outstretched arm.

"A box of apples, and an hour off from his labors."

"You traded him his clothes for lunch?"

"An extra hour," Orvalus explained, and handed Jessica the boots.

"They are… filthy. Orvalus…?" Jessica could not hide her disdain.

Orvalus took the clothes back and searched for the left wrist on the jumpsuit. Upon it he found a small red button and pressed. The jumpsuit sprang into full shape, like a car airbag inflating during a collision. The oil and mud fell solidly to the floor, with another insect similarly scurrying away into the library. Jessica stepped back in surprise. Orvalus handed it back to her, and she took it, amazed at the sudden transformation.

"That is cool!" Jessica remarked, and smelled the jumpsuit. "It's April fresh."

"What does the month of manufacture have to do with its olfactory appeal?" asked Dee, now coming from Orvalus's wrist.

Jessica shook her head dismissively. "It's advertising," she quickly thought about having to explain it. "Don't worry about it, it's a Terran custom." Happy with herself in using the Latinized form without being prompted, she asked "How does this work?" She turned the suit over in her hands, examining all the seams.

"Nano fiber," Orvalus explained. "The cloth returns to its manufactured form when a current is applied to it. How do you clean clothes?" He reached down to the boots and similarly pressed buttons on both, they shed their mud and water as quickly.

"We use a lot of water and soap." She glanced back up at Orvalus, trying to discern if he understood what she meant; then back at the boots. The water and mud had disappeared from the floor.

"That is wasteful," he said. "Put these on, we have much to do."

Jessica held up the jumpsuit, it was several sizes larger than she needed. "Is there a button for *this*?" she asked, craning her head around the suit at Orvalus.

"No, there is no way to… decrease the mass of the suit. You will have to make do."

Jessica shrugged and threw the jumpsuit on over her sweat clothes. She stood up; the suit bulged and pressed in odd places, which made her self-conscious of the whole affair. "How do I look?" She asked, holding her arms out like the Vitruvian Man.

"Acceptable," Orvalus said as he reached into his pocket to pull out a pair of sunglasses. He tossed them to Jessica. "These should conform to your face. Keep the hood up."

Jessica took the pair of black sunglasses and put them on. Designed for wearers without external ears, they immediately slipped off her face. On the second attempt, they held on tighter, and within moments felt as lightweight as any frames she had worn before.

"I can't see myself," she stated. At the phrase, the large display panel switched to a display of her, she turned toward it and regarded her projection.

"You will do well. Most of The People will not recognize you for a Terran."

Jessica thought the disguise could work. Maybe she could look like an alien child, but her only reference for comparison was Orvalus. She took one last look at her projection, and her insides squirmed, not from trans-dimensional warping, but nearly overwhelming anxiety. Taking a slow breath, she steadied herself, and her muscles relaxed, if only slightly.

"Okay," she said, pulling the hood up over her head. "I'm ready."

Chapter 12: Peek and Poke

They stepped out into the brilliant white sunlight and Jessica shielded her eyes with her hand. The sun shone brighter than she remembered from the last "version" of Bellerophon, with less smoke in the air. The air smelled less clean, with none of the pine she found comforting from the earlier iteration, or was it two iterations ago? She was already losing track. Keeping all this versioning in her memories proved difficult for her, like putting down a book and forgetting to leave a bookmark. Now with the knowledge of an infinity of such worlds, she tried not to think of it. A blustery breeze blew, and Jessica pulled at her hood to keep it secure.

"This is the only stable version of Bellerophon? All the others were unstable?"

"Yes," said Dee from Orvalus's wrist. "This version, the one we call Prime, is the one iteration in all of infinity that is habitable."

"In infinity? How can you say that? There must be other ones you don't know about."

"Yes, Terran, the gate network is capable of linking the infinity of the multiverse. We have not done so yet."

"You'd need infinite energy," Jessica said, stepping into the street, following Orvalus's lead.

"Yes, that is correct."

Jessica dodged an air-car hovering above the ground, which headed toward her much faster than any cab on Broadway. She shook from the near collision.

"They cannot harm you." Orvalus commented, seeing her apprehension. "They have… avoidance systems. It would have stopped."

She could not shake decades of dodging taxis, even self-driving ones, and trust the drivers on an alien planet.

They continued, stepping up onto the sidewalk. Jessica walked among what she discerned must have been androids. She wondered if Dee's other parts had similar appearances.

People and androids of all shapes and sizes strolled the avenue.

For the most part they were all silently communicating with each other with one data device or another, worn on their eyes, ears, and sometimes noses. Lights and amber LEDs lit the sidewalks in regular intervals. People barely paid attention to their surroundings. Something had to be guiding them, she surmised. AI interfaces were everywhere, their amber lights blinking slowly. Air-cars and The People danced around each other, connected and yet separate. It reminded her so much of midtown during the middle of the day - chaotic, stimulating, and terrifying. She smiled at the similarities, yet it saddened her as she longed for home even more. It didn't smell like home: concrete, car exhaust, burnt pretzels, falafel, and the occasional garbage dumpster. It all made her feel more alien than she ever had in her life.

Orvalus's huge steps had Jessica constantly hurrying to keep up, like a duckling running behind its mother. Moving past a collection of androids and small children, Jessica smiled to herself, despite her determination to be as nondescript as possible and not give away her alien status. The children were playing a game with the androids, she guessed from the laughter, but could not figure out the rules or the objective. They stood still and moved their faces slowly. It made no sense to her.

As Jessica strode by, the children did not notice her presence as they celebrated yet another win. Once she passed, two of the androids glanced away from their group and watched her leave. One android that bore whiskers flashed them blue and white, with a downward cast. A second later the androids were both staring back at the children who insisted they were not paying attention.

"Are there People in other dimensions you are still in contact with?" Jessica turned as Orvalus directed them down a smaller street off the main avenue. The street felt quieter and the buildings were less of the multicolored circus that barraged the senses of passersby.

"Yes, Terran, three colony worlds of The People are still connected to the network. They are not versions of Bellerophon, but separate worlds in their own right," Dee answered.

Jessica could feel her brain straining at the thought of having colonies in different dimensions. How did they stay connected? Was the culture of The People a true hegemony or were they fooling themselves?

Orvalus stopped in front of a narrow building, featureless except for a singular door and text scrawled above it. It started with a triangle and then the words, "City Networking and Data Retrieval Services."

"What does the triangle mean?" she asked out loud, remembering a similar triangle on the lintel of the door in the last version of Bellerophon, the one with the destroyed city. "I can't read it."

"It is… a pictogram. It means, 'storage,'" Orvalus said, as he pressed his hand against the door.

The door glowed amber, then opened from the bottom to the top, sliding noiselessly into the lintel.

"Come in, they are expecting us."

Jessica stepped into the room, right behind Orvalus, and immediately regretted the decision. It smelled like antiseptic circuit boards. The freezing cold assaulted her senses and the red light on her jumper's left wrist flashed. She pressed it and her suit started to warm.

She turned around quickly and saw dozens, if not hundreds, of plastic boxes filled with library cartridges. An entire wall festooned in receptacles, some filled and blinking, others completely empty. Cartridges were stacked in columns whose height made her feel uncomfortable. There also appeared to be no obvious organization for any of it. In many ways it resembled The Library, but in none of the more pleasant aspects. It gave off an industrial feel; this functioned as a working office, and the librarian was nowhere to be seen.

"Why are we here?" Jessica asked Orvalus.

"My associates work for the Administrator. They will help us in dealing with her."

Jessica surveyed the room, expecting to see the workstations for multiple people, but it appeared as if there was only one. Her eyebrow raised.

Orvalus scanned the room as well. "It would be best if we did not disturb anything. It might… upset them."

"Upset them? This disorder would upset anyone with a brain!" Dee chimed in, not hiding its disdain for the lack of what it considered organization.

"Not everyone goes about the world as you intend," Orvalus spoke into the air.

A moment later, another door on the far side of the room slid open, bright light flooded the office, and another alien, taller and thinner than Orvalus stepped through. It had the same pale grey skin as the bulkier alien and wore a green jumper. On its right temple three amber LEDs, arranged in a crescent moon shape, flashed in a random pattern.

Orvalus bowed at the figure's entrance, and it immediately bowed back. "It is good to see you again!" he intoned, with a broad smile.

"It's been a while." The other alien smiled quickly and nodded; the LEDs flashed a bright, solid amber. "So, this is the Terran?" the alien said quickly, turning toward Jessica but not looking directly at her, without a hint of pause.

I thought I was Orvalus's niece? Jessica thought to herself, wondering why the ruse was needed if the first person they met gave away the goose.

"Yes, it is. May I present Jessica Chao of Terra. Jessica, these are my... associates, Poke and Peek." Orvalus made the introductions, gesturing to the other alien.

Jessica looked quickly for the other of the pair, but saw none. She bowed reflexively, like being introduced to one of her mother's family members.

The LEDs on the figure's temple glowed rhythmically from top to bottom. "Peek says you have good manners. It likes it," Poke spoke to Jessica with a sideways glance, as if trying to not stare her directly in the eyes.

"Thank — Thank you... it?" Jessica flushed red with embarrassment. The LEDs flashed rhythmically, skipping the second light in the series each time.

"You're welcome."

Jessica shook her head quickly, attempting to grasp the situation,

"I'm sorry, which… who?"

Poke snorted quickly and smiled. "Peek is my companion." He gestured to his temple at the LEDs which burned a solid amber. "It's my symbiotic emulant AI."

Jessica stepped back and turned to Orvalus, who smiled down at her, then back at the "pair."

"You're a cyborg?"

Poke laughed timidly for a moment and glanced back and forth. The LED, Peek, flashed wildly. "No, I'm not. I don't need Peek, and Peek doesn't need me to live either."

"I'm sorry," Jessica said, a shot of electric embarrassment flooding her, "it's nice to meet you." She bowed again. Peek repeated the pattern.

"It's… all right?" Poke said, using the Terran turn of phrase. "You're not from here, obviously." Poke laughed nervously again.

"Yes," Jessica said, she wasn't intimidated, just confused. *How does it know slang?*

"Administrator Dux is busy," Poke said, turning toward Orvalus. "How do you expect us to do this? Why should she listen to you?" Peek flashed rhythmically again, like a cat flopping its tail, Jessica started to mentally assign it as a purr.

"My idea," Orvalus began, "is to give the Administrator something that she does not currently have, a reason to come to Bellerophon instead of Atlantis, and our new friend is proof that we have a reason."

Poke nodded quickly as he spoke, but Jessica thought he struggled with something.

"Well, I'm not sure…" Poke said after Orvalus finished speaking. "What if we get caught? Dee is supposed to report this to KT right away and hasn't. It could already be in trouble." Poke paused. "I know you're bored, but we have work to do. You see all the boxes, right?"

Unsure of whom Poke addressed, Jessica nervously answered, "Yes."

Poke turned in her direction, with Peek flashing wildly from his temple. "I was talking to Peek." Then he pointed to his head.

Jessica nodded her head yes quickly. This… person was strange, like one of the guys in her physics class who was both incredibly smart and socially awkward. Having someone else living in your head must be maddening, like being hooked into a cellphone all the time. How could he stand it?

"Right, but…" Poke faced the floor. "But what about what I want? Do you want to go back into the network permanently? I know you like it here."

Peek's LED lights went completely dark, and Poke shuddered. He threw his hands out, acting as if he were about to fall off a high place.

"Hey! That's not fair!" Poke reached behind himself and felt the surface of his desk. He sat back on it, the creak of the wood filling the room.

Jessica turned away from the pair, embarrassed to be witnessing a fight between two people she had just met, and attempted to give them their privacy. She couldn't understand why Orvalus still looked directly at them. She grabbed his wrist and gestured for him to avert his eyes. Orvalus smiled at her, then pointed to his own eyes.

Jessica glanced back at Poke and saw him surveying the office, but not focusing on anything, while Peek slowly brightened. She knew the behavior, and she turned back to Orvalus and whispered, "He's blind?" Orvalus nodded.

Suffering from strabismus and partial blindness in her own right eye, Jessica instantly understood his struggle. Out of respect, she still averted her eyes until he finished his internal dialogue. She knew how she wanted to be treated when she was practically staring at her own nose and attempting to be taken seriously. So, she decided to treat these exchanges as if the person were involved in a phone conversation, and nothing more.

"Fine," Poke said, and Peek switched to the content pattern. Poke addressed the others, "We'll help. But if this gets us in trouble, it's Peek's fault." He smiled weakly.

Chapter 13: Two Aliens, Two AI, and a Terran Walk into a Building

Upon stepping back out into the city, Jessica felt the breeze blowing considerably stronger than when they entered. The People hardly noticed, and yet were bundled up more tightly than they were a few minutes ago. Jessica pulled her hood down tighter over her head, and pressed her sunglasses tighter onto her face.

"Is it always this windy?" she asked. "I don't remember the other versions like this one."

"Versions?" Poke asked, with Peek flashing along.

"I was in different versions of Bellerophon before I got to this one. I don't remember a breeze at all."

"She is referring to the… Meridien wind," Orvalus prompted.

"Yeah. Uh. It's breezy like this every morning around eleven hundred hours. It starts cooling off for the day."

Jessica, used to winters in New York City, felt unusually chilly on this planet. The jumper and hoodie were barely providing enough heat to keep her warm, and she pressed the button on her left wrist to turn the heater back on.

"Cooling? Is it winter now?" she asked, fighting off a shiver.

"Winter?" asked Poke as he dodged an air-car and hopped up on the sidewalk, following Orvalus, although he didn't face in the direction of the car.

"The seasons, the part of the year where it gets colder than the rest," Jessica explained.

Poke cast his head down as they were walking, while Peek glowed a solid amber. After a moment he said, "Oh yes, 'winter.' There is no winter here. The temperature is the same daily."

"But I saw snow in the other versions. Where did it all go?" She asked, almost afraid to hear the answer, and she silently hoped it wouldn't be climate change like they were facing on her homeworld. She didn't like being cold all the time, but the end of winter could not be a good thing. She hoped this culture, with its obviously advanced technology, never went down that destructive path.

"Snow? Oh yes, snow. The city is shielded from frozen precipitation and extreme heat." Poke stopped walking and pointed to the sky.

Jessica followed his arm and scanned the gaps between the buildings. Above them she could see the faintest blue haze, like peering through a soap bubble. It swirled and undulated like the same, with a purplish iridescence.

"There is snow, there. On the mountains," he explained, pointing firmly.

Jessica strained to see what he was talking about, and only saw building and sky. Orvalus stepped in behind her, physically pushing her to the side. She craned her neck and could make out a small hint of a white-capped mountain in the distance. As she tried to get a better view, she bumped an android walking in the opposite direction. It stopped instantly and addressed her in Standard.

"Are you all right? Do you require any assistance?" Its gold-irised eyes focused on her, unblinking. The voice was not cold and robotic as she'd expected, but rather warm and comforting. Reflexively she leaned back and stared at it, desperately trying to mouth a response. She merely squeaked out, "Uh. Mm."

In a flash, the android's hands were up in front of her face, to which she stepped back in shock at the suddenness of it. Through the sunglasses she saw it trying to communicate with her in sign language. It signed, and spoke at the same time, "Miss, you well?" And then it continued explaining, "Your skin is dark. You appear ill. Would you like me to call for the medics?"

Orvalus immediately stepped between the two of them.

"There is no need for that, friend. My… niece, is from Atlantis, and she is not adapted to the cold of our planet. I can assure you, she is in perfect health, but not expecting the… Meridien to be so strong. Thank you for your concern." He smiled and wrapped his arm around Jessica's petite shoulders.

"Ah, I understand," the android said, its tone continuing to be congenial, but incrementally louder, as if she were also deaf. "Welcome to our planet, young miss. I trust you will find your stay stimulating and relaxing. Your uncle protects you well. Please call upon any of us if you need any assistance at all."

The lifeless face of the android stared at her impassively, which acutely juxtaposed to the geniality of its voice. Her first conversation with an android left her at a loss of how to respond. She merely nodded. Orvalus's fingers closed down on her shoulder, trying to calm her.

"I bid you good day, all," the android said, and then promptly turned and headed on its original path.

Dee spoke up from Orvalus's wrist, lacking any of the warmth of the other AI. "You need to be more careful, Terran. Fortunately, Orvalus stepped in to protect you."

"Uh, thanks?" she said, annoyance lacing her words.

"It is fine. She needs to learn how… helpful some of the *de novo* AI are, and how to respond appropriately."

Poke smiled at the dig, and Peek flashed brightly three times, laughing.

"There it is." Poke pointed again, this time down the street toward the corner. Under the common ceiling of the city blocks, emerged the spire of the Central Administration building. The building rose higher and higher until its white plastic edifice merged with the roof. White sunlight from a cross street cast upon it, and it glowed with an ethereal light.

Jessica regarded it with a bit of awe; it wasn't exactly the Empire State building at sunset, but the presentation impressed. They turned into the cross street and the change in orientation of the grid funneled the Meridien wind with sudden intensity. Jessica's hood caught it and it flew off her head, her dark brown hair, replete with green highlights, blew free in the strong gale. Instinctually, she threw up her hands and stuffed her mane back in as quickly as she could, before other "helpful" AI could render assistance. She stopped and glanced around, but no one had noticed. When her heart stopped thudding, she crossed the street with the rest of the group.

The open space across from the building was a welcome sight. The common ceiling felt claustrophobic to her, even more so than midtown Manhattan. At least there you could still see the sky over the buildings; from here all the buildings enclosed the streets, like a series of steel caves.

The building itself was featureless, smooth, and white with two entrances on the front of the building, both framed with amber lights. The larger, business entrance was choked with The People going to and fro. To the right, a smaller visitor's entrance appeared to be an afterthought.

"That is our entrance," Orvalus spoke to Jessica, pointing to the smaller door, "Is everyone prepared?"

"Yes," Jessica said with trepidation, "ready as I'll ever be."

Orvalus smiled as he stepped into the street, "Everything will be fine."

Chapter 14: The Ivory Tower

"Do you have a pass to see the administrator today?" asked the amber light of the door AI.

Jessica felt keenly aware of how the group around her must have appeared: the massive frame of Orvalus, the thin Poke, her childlike shape, disembodied voices everywhere. Yet, contrary to what she thought, the passersby barely took notice.

"I am Orvalus, Keeper of the Terran Gate, adjutant to D417a. I do not need a… pass to see the Administrator," Orvalus said sternly to the light panel, which pulsed quiescently.

Poke stepped away from Orvalus's right side and took up a position behind Jessica.

"I hate when he gets 'official,'" he whispered to her. Jessica nodded in acknowledgment, but disagreed entirely.

"I am aware of your rank, Orvalus, Keeper of the Terran Gate, but the administrator is a busy personage and you do not have a pass, nor is her schedule clear to receive visitors." The door spoke back to him in its emotionless voice.

Dee jumped into the conversation from Orvalus's wrist, its voice rising with indignation,

"I am D417a, Liaison to KT, Overseer of the Terran Gate, Vice Assistant to the Order of The Network, Prelate of the…" It carried on and on for a minute listing ranks and honorifics. Jessica turned back at Poke and raised her eyebrows, moving her sunglasses up. Peek flashed in sequence from Poke's temple; she could tell it was amused. After Dee's oral record finished, the door responded, again coolly.

"I understand, Liaison D417a. The Administrator is still far too busy today. Would you like to schedule an appointment to see her? She has an opening for fifteen minutes, two weeks from tomorrow. Will that be satisfactory?"

"Well, I…" Dee's voice cut off, Peek's three lights flashed a solid amber and stayed there.

"That will be… acceptable. Please make the appointment and add it to my calendar," Orvalus responded, then turned to the others.

"Come, children, let us go about our day." Determination grew across his face.

Poke growled at the reference to being called a child. Jessica felt bad for him and debated putting a consoling arm around his shoulder. Still unfamiliar with the customs of this world, she decided it would be better not to, lest she inadvertently offend him.

Orvalus walked straight out into the traffic of the busy street, disregarding the cars and pedestrians who gave him a wide berth. Jessica and Poke did their best to stay in his wake as they followed. When they finally crossed, they entered a small park; purple pine trees and grass filled the small square. Orvalus, without checking, sat down and a plastic chair arose from the ground to meet him.

"What we need," he said, fixing his gaze on the Central Administration building, "is a way to get on her schedule before those two weeks."

"Is there some way to get on her schedule? Can we talk to someone and convince them?" Jessica asked into the air, also staring at the building.

"We have already spoken to the highest person responsible for her scheduling, Terran," Dee remarked.

Poke's temple flashed, solid, then the glowing purr pattern.

"Really?" Poke spoke to Peek out loud so that the others might hear. "Peek is friends with an AI which has access to the scheduling mainframe." He stood motionless as the amber lights flashed in his temple, staring into space as if lost in thought, occasionally muttering to himself.

The other two gave him his reverie, anticipating his return. Dee remained silent.

"Right… so, Peek already asked, and they gave him access." Poke shifted his feet a bit and squared his shoulders. "But it's Group Six access, and we need Group Seven. It would require us to, you know, forge Group Seven access. Which is, kinda… illegal."

Orvalus stood up from the chair, which immediately dissolved into the ground. Dee chimed in immediately.

"No. I strictly forbid it."

Orvalus grimaced. "Dee, we cannot wait around for two weeks for her schedule to clear up. Do you want to wait and not report to KT? You yourself said this would be an opportunity to learn about Terran culture. If you are willing to bend the rules for knowledge, why would you… hesitate from doing so now?"

"This is a slippery slope into anarchy. Laws are there for a reason. I order you to not do this."

Orvalus closed his eyes and breathed slowly. His right fist clenched.

Jessica turned to Poke. "Poke, who do you and Peek work for?"

Poke perked up. "We work for the Central Network Library of Bellerophon City," he said with pride.

"Dee is not your overseer?" she inquired, leading the questioning. Orvalus broke into a grin, nodding his head slowly.

"No, friend Jessica, we don't work for Dee," Poke answered with finality. Peek flashed in sequence from bottom to top, again amused.

"Can you do me a favor, then?" she asked.

Peek lit up, fully solid.

"Already happening," Poke responded.

"This is not… You are guilty of a crime. All of you." Dee sputtered from Orvalus's wrist.

"Arrest us, then. Explain how you aren't part of a group of law-breakers harboring an alien." Jessica shot back, her face white-hot with anger. She shook at the sudden rage, and frightened herself with her flippant response.

"Noted, Terran. I am not happy about this."

Jessica nodded in acknowledgment. Orvalus desperately tried to not laugh, his rising chest betraying his attempt.

"Ha!" Poke interjected. "Peek is in and forged us access. We are so gonna get busted for this."

Orvalus chided, "We do not need to draw unnecessary attention to us. Please… refrain from doing so in the future."

Poke immediately dropped his gaze and tilted his head toward the ground.

Peek flashed amused again, and Poke translated, "We can move into her slot in a few hours or take the one first thing in the morning."

"Do not give her time to prepare for our arrival. Schedule for the next one."

Poke nodded and Peek flashed quickly. In a few moments he responded, "We are in."

Jessica sighed in relief, and felt butterflies tangle her stomach at the same time. She had no idea if this person would help her at all or send her on her way. She could only hope.

In the intervening hours, Jessica spent as much time as she could studying the scenery and culture. The People acted so much like New Yorkers to her, always going someplace, always something needing to be done. Yet, distinctly, they had less of the angst about them. They were busy, but not overwhelmed like so many people she knew, including herself.

"How many people live here?" she asked Orvalus, who'd come back from a food vendor with fruits she had never seen before. She ate a purple one resembling a strawberry but tasted of bananas.

"Approximately fifteen million Takki, and two hundred million AI."

"Takki?" she asked, opening yet another peach-like fruit. This one smelled of parsley.

"Ah yes, the Takki, the biological part of The People," he said, pointing to himself, while he opened a melon nearly identical to a watermelon, with insides unmistakably pumpkin.

Jessica leaned across and smelled the fruit. *Cinnamon again*, she thought to herself.

"This is but a provincial city compared to the other worlds. Atlantis holds sixty million Takki in the capital city alone."

Jessica's mind boggled at the scale, the largest city she had ever been in was Shanghai at twenty-five million.

"And AI?" she inquired.

"Four hundred eighteen million, six hundred fifty-eight thousand, three hundred four." Dee paused for a moment, "Nine hundred eighty-one have just come online."

Orvalus's wrist display flashed green, and he held it up to his face. "It is time."

Chapter 15: Administrator Dux

The group crossed the street again, since the early afternoon chaos had abated somewhat, and it was easier to stay in Orvalus's wake this time.

"Ah, you have returned. Good to see you again," the door AI chimed, without adding emotion to its otherwise cheerful greeting.

"We have an appointment with Administrator Dux. Please allow us entry."

"As I have stated before, Gatekeeper Orvalus, the Administrator…" the door trailed off.

Poke held his breath, and Peek's lights faded to barely visible.

"… has had an opening and you have been placed into the queue quite ahead of schedule. She must want to see you with equal exigency."

At the end of its sentence, the door immediately opened, silently splitting in half, revealing a stark white hallway inside.

"Enjoy your day," the door spoke, again with no emotion.

Her tension rising to unbearable levels, Jessica blurted out, "Thank you, you too!" to the door, which took no notice of her benediction. Her response drew a gasp from Poke, and Orvalus glared down at her. She shrunk a bit, and waited for Orvalus to step into the hallway before she followed him.

"Children do not speak unless spoken to," he chided once they had all stepped into the hallway and the door closed solidly behind them.

"Sorry, I…"

"You still have much to learn, Jessica," he said, a particularly paternal tone in his voice.

The three walked down the white hallway; gently curving walls arched up to a vaulted ceiling. Orange light, cast by sconces high on the walls, gave the passage a feeling of being in a forest at sunset. The air felt cool and fresh. The sounds of their footfalls echoed off the walls, not harsh, but a full octave lower than the actual sound. Music drifted softly through the air, light and airy, yet nothing Jessica had ever heard before.

"I feel like I'm in a church," Jessica commented to herself, aloud.

Poke chuckled after Peek told him what the word "church" meant. "A shrine to administration," he joked.

Jessica laughed despite - or because of - her anxiety.

Dee chimed in from Orvalus's wrist, "The Central Administration building is designed to show The People of the simplicity and elegance of order. Everything in this building is organized, minimalist, and beautiful."

"This place is… too clean," Orvalus whispered, as if the elegance forbade him to speak loudly.

At the end of the hallway stood a single orange door. Surrounded by the creamy white of the walls, Jessica instantly remembered an orange creamsicle, her favorite ice cream.

The door did not immediately open, nor did it have an obvious way to access the room beyond. They stopped and waited.

Orvalus shifted his weight. Jessica stared up at the ceiling. Peek flashed rhythmically on Poke's temple, and he turned distractedly away, having an internal conversation only the two of them understood. The music changed to another piece, quieter and more restful than the previous one.

Stifling a yawn, Jessica whispered, "I thought this person was busy? What gives?"

"I do not know," Orvalus whispered back, then to the air, "Administrator Dux, we have arrived."

No response. Poke blinked his eyes, fighting off the quiet.

"Administrator?" Orvalus inquired again.

From the air around them, above the level of the music, a voice responded.

"Yes, just a moment."

Dee said, "That is she."

"Peek, what did you tell her we were here to see her for?" Orvalus asked.

Peek flashed for a moment and Poke translated. "It told them to say were presenting ideas to get more visitors to Bellerophon. Nothing more."

"Interesting that she found it so… urgent, and now she makes us wait."

The three stood there, examining the simple detailing on the doors. The ceiling lights changed from orange to a soft purple so slowly as to be imperceptible. Jessica's eyes closed and her head drifted down slowly.

"Administrator?" Dee asked.

"Yes, one moment."

Jessica's head shot up to meet Orvalus's similar sleepy expression. He shook his head and cleared his throat.

Again, they waited.

"How long have we been waiting?" Jessica asked after a moment.

"Fourteen minutes, thirty-six seconds. Nearly the entire time of our appointment," Dee commented.

Jessica felt butterflies gathering in her stomach, the anticipation piquing in her.

"Administrator Dux?" She spoke into the air, violating the warning she received earlier from Orvalus about "children" not speaking out of turn.

"Yes, please come in."

The creamsicle door clicked and opened slowly. The air felt stuffy and warm, and the sounds of fans filled the room. A mother-of-pearl desk, stacked with papers, display cards, cartridges, and empty food plates stood directly in front of them. To their left, a massive display took up the entire wall, the display further broke down into individual windows, each showing a different display of innumerable tables, charts, and graphs, all updated every few seconds. To the right, the wall bristled with cartridge readers, keyboards, and amber AI interfaces, some of which were actively communicating. The three stood there taking in the overwhelming display.

"Administrator?" Jessica asked again, disregarding any previous proscription.

"Yes!" The tall, slender form of Administrator Dux stood up from behind the desk. She wore glasses, one lens containing an amber display; a speaker nestled in her left ear, and a slender microphone tapered from the earpiece and ended at the tip of her elegantly pointed chin. She pocketed a tablet into her orange coat, and smoothed it down to her lavender trousers. Her pale grey skin and emerald eyes strained, but regained composure rapidly.

She cleared her throat. "Forgive me, I dropped this," she spoke as she patted the tablet in her pocket.

"Administrator," Orvalus intoned, and bowed at the waist, the other two in the party followed suit.

"Gatekeeper Orvalus, good to see you again," she nodded to the large Takki, "and to you, D417a."

"It is agreeable to be in your presence," Dee responded without emotion.

She scanned Poke, and nodded politely. "Hello, Poke and Peek." She turned her gaze to Jessica. "And whom do we have here?"

Orvalus stepped forward, gesturing to Jessica.

"Administrator, allow me to introduce…" he hesitated, backed away from the ruse of her being his niece, and simply went with, "Jessica."

"A pleasure to meet you, Administrator." She thought desperately how to be less serious, fearing the formality would give her away. "I… love your desk." She instantly regretted speaking.

The right side of the administrator's mouth pulled back into a smile, which she quickly stopped. "Thank you. You have good taste, young one. Please sit."

Jessica's face flashed hot, and the cool air radiating in from the hallway did little to cool her down. She felt sweat forming on the small of her back. The trio took seats that grew up from the floor.

Orvalus spoke. "Administrator, we have come here seeking your advice on opening the Terran Gate. What we are proposing is not allowed and we cannot assume to have any help. We think this will be advantageous for you and your administration, but it requires some risk. We are requesting your clemency." He voiced his lines with some trepidation, as if he had rehearsed them over and over, and with the final performance, was unsure of the entire soliloquy.

Administrator Dux adopted a contrapposto pose and glanced back and forth between Orvalus and Jessica. Her eyes squinted, and her cheeks stiffened, then she relaxed.

"I see, and why do you need to do so? What have you done wrong?"

"What?" Orvalus stammered. "What?" he turned his attention back to Jessica, who felt the weight of all their gazes upon her. She wanted the help to get back home so badly she had never considered how she would ask for it, or to consider being taken at her word. She'd thought Orvalus would do all the talking, and now panicked at his inability to explain themselves. Now that she was here, and given the opportunity, she balked at having to use the agency given her.

Administrator Dux shifted again and took off her headset. She rubbed her eyes and drew a slow breath, then held her head up slowly. Fatigue showed on her face. Jessica sat still, unsure of what to do.

She moved from behind the desk and stood in front of them. Jessica regarded her elegant form, taller than her by a foot and a half, easily taller than Orvalus and Poke.

"Jessica is lucky," Administrator Dux stated, turning to Orvalus, "to have so many people willing to risk so much for her. However, when given the opportunity they must not falter in the face of authority."

Poke sat back quickly, confusion shooting across his face. Peek grew to solid intensity, all three LEDs blazing, then quickly dimming to their lowest.

The administrator turned her gaze back to Jessica. "I've never met a Terran before. It's a shame you want to return so quickly before we have had the chance to know anything about you."

Chapter 16: Quid Pro Quo

Jessica froze. Her hands and insides shook and tingled like fire, and she fought the urge to vomit.

Orvalus gibbered, "Administrator, I… we…"

Dee chimed from Orvalus's wrist, "I told you all this was a bad idea, did I not? Administrator, I expressly forbade them from exercising in this tomfoolery. I apologize, as Liaison to KT…"

The administrator cut it off. "You need to try harder if you intend to prove to me you are worthy of risking the lives of the entire Hegemony with opening the Terran Gate."

"I'm sorry, I think… well, you are intimidating if you don't already know that. How long have you known about me?" Jessica inquired.

"When someone with Group Six access suddenly becomes Group Nine. It's obvious not everything is as it seems."

Poke smiled sheepishly as Peek flashed like mad. Jessica gasped and threw an accusatory glance at the pair and mouthed *Nine?* Orvalus shook his head in frustration realizing Peek acted on its own and did exactly what they told the emulant not to do.

"Plus, I don't know of any one of The People to have hair, Takki or not." Administrator Dux reached under Jessica's hood and threw it back, exposing her green and brown shoulder-length locks.

"This is interesting."

Administrator Dux turned back around and sat behind her desk. She lifted a display pad and pressed a few buttons; the giant display showed the group leaving Poke and Peek's office. The breeze blew Jessica's hood off before she quickly pulled it back over.

Administrator Dux shut the display off and brightened the lights in the room to their maximum. The amber AI connections shut off instantly. "I know what I can do for you in this situation. My question is, what can you do for me?"

Jessica sat back, unsettled by the quick dealing. Again, the brass ring had been presented before her, and she responded simply and honestly. "I just want to go home Ma'am. I don't have anything to offer except my knowledge: I study physics. I speak a few languages, badly, and am a hard worker."

Orvalus broke into the conversation. "Administrator, you and I are very aware Bellerophon is a backwater research city." She bristled at Orvalus's admission, he continued. "I mean no disrespect, as many of us feel… comfortable with the situation. However, we can be so much more."

Administrator Dux sat back in her chair, and steepled her fingers. Her eyes narrowed slightly. Orvalus continued.

"Atlantis is the administrative center of this sector, the heart and soul of the system. Bellerophon is a large research center, yes; however, if you are not actively studying, you have no reason to be here."

"And opening the Terran Gate, if stable, would give you more than an academic reason to be here?" The administrator led him with a thinly veiled pun.

"Yes, Administrator, Atlantis prospers because it is connected to four trans-dimensional gates as well as six others within the Hegemony in this dimension. One arrives at Atlantis with a place to go; Bellerophon is the destination."

Jessica sat back and watched the normally terse Orvalus wax poetic about his world, his biased assessment stood out as he spoke. All the trepidation and anxiety he displayed before now completely gone. Jessica agreed with his train of thought. All the largest cities on Earth were gateways: New York, London, Shanghai, Tokyo, Lagos, even Ancient Rome and Istanbul. Singapore began as a sleepy fishing village before it transformed itself into a commercial hub. Connections drove commerce and tourism, and these places prospered by either being in the right place at the right time, or were designed specifically to be so. She admired his determination and maneuvering.

After Orvalus finished he sat quietly, letting the administrator ruminate on his disquisition. Poke lost all interest and spoke with Peek inside his head, and Dee was curiously silent.

"And you see your position as Keeper of the Terran Gate as central to this plan of a new gateway, with you as the controller?" Administrator Dux interrogated coolly.

"I would not be so presumptuous, Administrator. I am merely D417a's adjutant. It would prosper from the position more than I."

Dee finally chimed in. "I would serve as Liaison to the best of my programming. I see it as an intellectual challenge. Having visited Terra in the past, I would be uniquely qualified for such a position. Their culture is primitive and barbaric, barely above animals."

Jessica chafed at the reference to a primitive society again, but felt it better not to interrupt.

Dee continued, "Obviously, they have attained much since the last time we have encountered them. Even in their rude state, we could benefit from study. If they have advanced sufficiently enough to develop gate technology on their own, it would behoove us to guide them in its proper use, lest they become a direct adversary. I have no ego driving me for anything other than to serve The People and ensure the security of the Hegemony."

The Administrator's lip curled upward, "Likely."

She relaxed her fingers, and tapped on her tablet, paused to read something quickly, then turned back to the trio. Before she spoke, she glanced down at the tablet again, then back up.

"How do you all plan to convince KT to allow this highly unusual request? It is tasked with keeping the network stable, and you are asking it to re-open a gate to a world closed for that very reason. You know the law better than anyone else. You have not reported a breech in gate integrity. You've let an unauthorized alien walk our streets and interact with The People. You have started into this affair with breaking the rules and now ask to break them further? What am I missing here? How can we ask for such a thing after all this?"

"And not put your position on the line?" Jessica interrupted.

"Yes, my position," she responded without malice.

"Send me back though the gate, let me show you we are safe, and our world isn't as barbaric and backward as you remember. If I can give you proof it is worth it, we should be able to convince KT. Trade, research, or if you want to gawk at the primitives. If it is stable." Jessica betted with cards she did not have, and she knew it. What choice did she have?

"If." The Administrator paused, picked up a display card and typed something, then closed the screen. She took a breath and then continued. "A compelling argument, Terran, but what assurances will I have you won't simply disappear once you make it back to your homeworld? Once you got what you wanted, why would you come back? You would only prove your barbarism and penchant for deception."

Jessica couldn't respond. The administrator was correct; once she got back home, Jessica could do whatever she wanted. Closing the gate at that time would mean nothing to her.

"You gamble well, until it is your turn to bet." Administrator Dux stood up, and the trio likewise stood.

"You will take D417a, as well as Poke and Peek, with you. You will all enter the Terran Gate at the same time, and you will return together in unison. If you do not, the gate will not be reopened, and they will not be able to return. You will trap them there, as you are trapped here."

Poke immediately shook his head "no" again. Dee made no comment.

"Ma'am, I can't ask them to do that. It's not worth it. I can't…"

"You are not asking them, Terran. I am ordering it."

Jessica quickly turned to Poke, who slowly closed his eyes. Peek pulsed, amused.

"What am I to do in this time?" Orvalus questioned, regarding his charge with concern.

"You are the Keeper of the Terran Gate. You will monitor them from this side. You will be responsible for allowing them to return. Is this acceptable to you, Liaison?"

Dee spoke from Orvalus's wrist. "Yes, Administrator."

"Good. Be prepared to leave by eighteen hundred hours this evening," she responded as she opened the creamsicle door.

"KT?" Poke asked as the trio walked toward the door.

"I will handle it."

Stepping through the threshold, Jessica turned back to see all the displays and AI screens in the office flood back into use. Administrator Dux put her headpiece on and turned her back to the door, typing furiously on her tablet. The lighting changed from purple back to orange.

"Okay then," Jessica said with a sigh, her hands shaking.

Chapter 17: The Ribbons

"So, how are we supposed to do all of this?" asked Poke, tapping the interface for Peek on his temple.

"You're my emo cousin Max from Taipei who has come to visit," answered Jessica, glancing up and down the tall Takki. "With a beanie and a hoodie, no one will even notice." She tapped her sunglasses as well.

"We need to retrieve my bodies from storage. I will blend in exactly as I did before," Dee said from Orvalus's wrist.

"Bodies? Plural?" Jessica inquired.

"Yes, bodies. I have several. Although I presume one or two heads will suffice."

Orvalus chuckled without comment.

"Orvalus knows the location. I will prepare them." The amber square disappeared from Orvalus's wrist.

"The location is across the city, and Dee does not require our assistance. However, I think we should go. We could summon an air-car, but we can have much more... fun this way. We can take the ribbons." Orvalus pointed to a set of stairs and elevators at the corner of the street, looking for all the world like the entrance to a subway.

"Do these go uptown or downtown?" Jessica quipped.

"The ribbons go anywhere in the city. The trick is... knowing when to jump," Orvalus said with a wink.

The three took the open elevator down to the ribbons. Miles and miles of moving walkways stretched throughout the bowels of the city. Moving at different speeds and at different heights, they were also color-coded and festooned with lights, flashing in different patterns to denote destination and speed, like airport people movers gone amok. The ribbons were filled with Takki and AI going about their day, some at a sedate rate, barely above a normal walk, others so fast as if to be a blur. Five times the amount of The People were using the ribbons than were walking on the streets above. There were no seats, no restraining devices, nothing save the moving walkway and the crush of bodies.

Jessica stared at it dumbfounded. Her breath quickened and her stomach knotted.

"Orvalus… I… can't," she gasped, clutching his arm, this was beyond her street smarts or athleticism.

"Yes, you can. I will be with you," he reassured her. Poke had already gone.

"That bastard," Jessica muttered under her breath. Orvalus laughed.

"Come, we will start off slowly."

Orvalus led her by the hand to the nearest ribbon, green and flat. It moved at a pace slower than walking. Filled with Takki children and small AI, Jessica felt both offended and thankful.

"Step onto the ribbon and keep your eyes down until you become accustomed to switching."

Jessica stepped onto the slow ribbon behind a group of children barely smaller than she. They glanced at her and gave her space, giggling all the while. Orvalus saw them and smiled.

"My niece is… from Atlantis," he explained and then glanced to the next ribbon which ran slightly faster, and up a foot. It had grey coloring and to Jessica's mind seemed the default speed for the system. She stabilized her feet, and nodded when Orvalus motioned to it with his chin.

Together, the two stepped up to the grey ribbon. It took a second for her to adapt to the speed, and they moved away from the children, who waved and giggled.

"Good!" The Gatekeeper grinned. "This is all about rhythms. Once you get the feel, you don't even need to watch."

Jessica laughed to herself, noting the older Takki standing on the ribbon next to her. They reminded Jessica of the older ladies in her neighborhood getting their morning coffee, out for the day with no plan or destination. They smiled pleasantly. Attempting to mimic the voice of her protector, she smiled back and explained.

"I am… not from around here."

To which the android behind her responded, "Do you require assistance, young miss?" Its gold-irised eyes stared at her impassively. This model possessed whiskers emerging from both sides of its face, less like those of a cat, and more like a halo. They pulsed a smooth blue and white.

Orvalus responded politely, "That will not be necessary, friend. She needs to learn on her own."

To which the android nodded, changing the color of its whiskers to solid green.

"Ready for the next one?" Orvalus pointed to another ribbon, which was brown and a foot to the right of the one they were on. It was a few inches higher up, and moving much faster.

Jessica felt a thrill of excitement, and stepped onto the brown ribbon without help, spinning her head back to encourage Orvalus along. He smiled and shook his head, and deftly sprang onto the ribbon. Then, without hesitating, stepped up to the next ribbon, a blue one, running alongside at the speed of a slow run. Jessica took a breath and jumped on, clutching at Orvalus's arm for stability. She smiled and laughed.

"Do you feel it? The rhythm? The speed changes between the colors?" The excitement grew in his voice.

"I do! This is cool!"

"You may not hear it yet, but the ribbons also change sound and vibration as they go. Try to feel it when you are comfortable."

Orvalus pointed ahead to an interchange, one ribbon passing below this one. Amber lights flooded the area, and AI and Takki deftly stepped from one to the other without incident. The butterflies in Jessica's stomach jumped into her throat, and she swallowed hard.

"You can do it. Watch the others, and remember where they jump. I will lead." Orvalus smiled and grabbed her hand. She felt completely at ease and trusted him. She off her anxiety as quickly as she could, and watched the others step between ribbons, counting in her mind.

In a flash, Orvalus called, "Now!"

In one deft jump, Orvalus and Jessica switched from her blue ribbon to a yellow one. Her head spun from the change in direction, and she felt her stomach lurch. Fluid and soft, unlike anything she had experienced before, she felt free, unbound by gravity, like a bird finally taking flight. She tried not to let the reality that this was the equivalent of taking the subway —minus the panhandlers— sink into her mind. She didn't want the feeling of freedom to be spoiled by the mundane.

"Good, we can wait on this one for a few minutes." Orvalus smiled.

Jessica caught her breath and took in the view; dozens of ribbons ran below her and still more, and even faster ones ran above her. Everyone stood nonchalant and casual as if they had been doing it all their lives. She felt her eye turning in toward her nose, and forced her eyes up toward her eyebrow to pull it into place. She blinked rapidly as her eyes refocused.

"How did Poke manage it? I don't see any disabled people."

"Ah, Poke is… more capable than you or I in negotiating the ribbons. Peek reads all the data and sends the necessary information to him. He could run these in the dark. There are assisted people here, look around."

Jessica scanned the ribbons. She had been moving too fast to see it before, but now that she was paying attention, she saw. A few Takki had artificial limbs, supportive braces, AI symbiotes, input devices, etc.

"Amazing. What if they don't want to use assistance?" She hoped that there wasn't an undercurrent of ableism on this world.

Orvalus was downcast. "No one forces them. If they require other assistance, then air-cars provide them transportation. Or… they are homebound." His voice drew off as he spoke the last words. He took a sharp breath. "We do not consider anyone of The People to be enabled or disabled. We are all one people with variations on the theme. Each makes their own way how they choose." He emphasized "they."

Jessica thought something more lurked behind his explanation than he let on. The feeling she had when she first saw the interaction between him and Poke. Again, she thought better than asking.

"We are reaching our jump-off point." Orvalus intoned, breaking her reverie, and pointed in the distance. There, Poke stood at the exit platform, patiently waiting.

"Jump?" Jessica asked, fighting back the lump in her throat.

"Relax, we do all of this in reverse."

The pair moved from the fast-moving ribbons to the slower ones in sequence. Each time Jessica felt like she was jumping from one river onto another, like a moving metallic parkour park. She smiled and laughed as each step changed her direction and speed. She didn't want it to end. When they alighted off the last ribbon, Jessica twirled and swung her arms out, nearly knocking a wayward child to the ground. She smiled and stabilized him.

"Thanks, kid!" he called and ran off with an android.

She giggled and took Orvalus's hand. "That was great! Thanks for taking me!"

He smiled down at her.

Poke walked up to them, and Peek flashed its purr.

"It's about time. I've been waiting forever," Poke quipped.

Jessica leaned forward and mockingly punched his shoulder.

The trio took the elevator back up to the midafternoon sunlight. The Meridien wind had abated for the day, and a cool breeze blew down the streets. There were considerably more AI than Takki, and the streets had a calmer, more orderly aspect. Jessica couldn't shake the uneasy feeling at the lack of organic-based life. Street after street was arranged in discretely neat blocks of uniform buildings. There was no public decoration. Not even a park. Everywhere amber lights blinked.

Jessica remarked about the dearth of ornamentation. "Pretty spartan, huh?"

"They do not feel the need for… superfluous adornments in this neighborhood," Orvalus responded.

Jessica wondered how the AI felt in more organic neighborhoods. In her hometown she blended in with everyone else, and no one noticed, or cared, how different you were. Here, a life form based on completely different chemistry filled the streets. She turned to watch Poke sauntering along beside her, Peek flicking away engaged in conversation in his mind. How they merged still astounded her. Not a cyborg, but not separate.

They turned a corner and passed through a large doorway in another nondescript building. This one was marked with another triangle, and the words read: "Accessories, Parts, Exosuits, Furnished and Reconditioned."

"It lives in a repair shop?"

"No, friend Jessica," Poke answered with Peek laughing, "it is the repair shop."

Chapter 18: The Android

The trio stepped into the workshop of D417a. Jessica gasped at the sight of the most well-ordered and clean warehouse she had ever seen and wondered if it was the most so ever imagined. Rows and rows of grey cabinets were stacked floor to ceiling. Some cabinets were a few feet on a side, others were more than six feet in height; all were glistening white and made from the same plastic material as the Central Administration building. The pattern repeated, like a three-dimensional black-and-white Mondrian, on an epic scale.

Each cabinet had a singular black display, about the size of a credit card. They blinked a serial number of twelve alphanumeric characters in either amber, green, or red. Jessica scanned the displays. Other than the color, none of them had any consistent numbering scheme she could discern.

There has to be a pattern, she thought to herself, and walked right up to the closest cabinet with a red display and pressed it. With a hiss, the cabinet slid open, rolling on silent coasters. Jessica stepped back and surveyed the contents. Wires and servos, impeccably arranged and cleaned, lined the bottom of the drawer. A faint smell of circuit cleaner and ozone filled the air.

"Please do not touch the storage lockers, Terran," Came Dee's voice, from everywhere. Louder than she had ever heard it before. With that, the cabinet closed noiselessly.

"I'm sorry Dee, I…"

"Didn't realize the consequence of your actions. A common trait among your species."

Jessica rolled her eyes, feeling like being caught peeking into her mom's bedroom.

"I like to think of it as curiosity," she retorted, running her gaze down the long axis of the room at a solid white wall.

"Curiosity is what stranded you here in the first place, and forced us on this course of action."

"This is… not constructive," Orvalus broke in, just as Jessica's hand raised into a pointed finger.

A silence fell over the room. The circulation pumps for the air system keeping the room cold provided the only sound. The wrist-light on Jessica's jumpsuit flashed, letting her know it could turn up the heat if needed.

"Right, so what do you do here?" Poke inquired.

"I am the Liaison to KT. Poke, this is not new information to you. This is where I catalogue and repair decommissioned hardware. I have other assigned duties than disseminating orders to Orvalus."

A door in the solid wall slid open, and out stepped a six-foot human. Jessica gasped. Olive skin and sandy blonde hair. Male in appearance, it resembled a Mediterranean male human in his mid-thirties. It had a medium build, and wore a hoodie and sweats similar to Jessica's. Pleasantly attractive, but not overly so. It surveyed the trio with gold-irised eyes, like all the other AI they had seen, but the irises were in human eyes. Jessica ran up, elated to see another of her kind, and only when she got two feet away did she catch her emotions.

"This is how you visited Earth?"

The android answered, "Terra. Yes, this is how I visited Terra."

It added a curious affectation of a smile. It didn't appear quite right to Jessica's eyes, but she could not place it. An example of "uncanny valley," the point at which the image of a human simulacrum becomes close enough to fully human, but not quite, leaving a sense of revulsion and fear. It appeared close, though, but the over emphasis of upturn betrayed the inhumanity. Dee's voice spoke through the face, and although she recognized it, it sounded softer and richer than before. As much as the face was a close approximation, the voice mimicked humanity unambiguously. She felt herself liking it.

"This isn't your body on Bellerophon, where is that one? You don't walk around looking like a human here." She questioned, not forgetting its mention of "multiple" bodies.

"Well remembered," it commented, and another door opened. A rack slid out from it, and on it an android body like all the ones she had seen hung from several bars. Sleek, brown, with amber lights. The head lacked many features, save for a mouth slot, two gold eyes eschewing sclera, and six whiskers arranged like a cat's. The eyes were dark, and the head hung in a low-power state. She scanned back and forth between Dee's two bodies and decided she liked the less human form better. Less to remember.

"When you said you wanted two heads, why this one?" She pointed to one on the rack.

"Are two heads not better than one?" it responded.

Poke chuckled at the AI using the Terran idiom.

"How often did you use this one on Ear… Terra?"

Dee gestured to the body on the rack. "When I was in the temple, I preferred this body. I always prefer this body. It uses less energy and has less subroutines to make it appear human."

"I can guarantee you, you will not need this body. I don't know of any robot-worshiping temple. You'd be so obvious."

"I am not a robot, I am an android," it spoke from the human head, a definite sense of pride in its voice.

"Either way, this body is going to get us in trouble. Leave it here."

Orvalus chuckled.

"Since you are the expert, I will do as you say, Terran. However, I still think it would be better for me to take both in case."

"Then it will be my fault, like the other stuff," she commented with a flippant air. "Does the body make you more biological and not such a dork all the time?" She knew she should not have said that, but could not resist the dig.

"Dork?"

She shook her head.

"Dee, may I?" Orvalus interjected

"Yes, you may. I have unlocked it for you."

Orvalus walked over to another cabinet on the first row of cabinets. He pressed a green display, and the drawer slid open. Removing a few artifacts, he placed them in his pockets and pushed the drawer closed.

Dee turned toward Jessica. "Peek cannot exist without a connection to the network. What you see is merely a relay between Poke's brain and its consciousness. It must be contained in a device for us to bring it along, one that would not arouse suspicion."

Orvalus raised his wristband that erstwhile contained Dee's interface.

"Why can't it live with you?" she asked, not understanding the technical details.

Peek flashed wildly and Poke suppressed a laugh.

"It would be… we cannot… it is not done," Dee explained, embarrassment in its voice.

"Why?" Jessica's forehead wrinkled.

"Sentient beings are not housed within each other, Terran, it is… abhorrent."

Jessica looked at Poke's temple where Peek still flashed its laugh sequence.

Poke answered her unvoiced question,

"Peek doesn't live here, it's merely the interface."

The intricacies of AI intimacy completely foiled her reasoning.

"There is already a solution." Dee pointed to Jessica's pocket.

"My phone?" she asked, patting the aluminum and glass smartphone in her pocket.

"Yes, the device is primitive, but it will serve our needs. We have already scanned it, and are aware of its limitations. Peek has already consented to using it."

Jessica felt uneasy, but being stranded in a foreign dimension, she was slowly starting to get used to not having control, or privacy. She took out the phone and pressed the unlock button. It was as dead now as before.

Chapter 19: The Silver Stone

Dee took the smartphone from Jessica and placed it in the nearest amber drawer. A new alphanumeric code appeared in the black space on the otherwise featureless surface.

"I have a lot of pictures in there. I kinda like them," Jessica explained.

"Do not worry, Terran, we can compress all the current data without affecting - my that is small storage space," Dee commented. Jessica turned her head to get a better view of it. Did it make a joke?

"This battery is very primitive as well. How can this device do anything worthwhile to your species?"

"I ask that a lot. Most people use them to text and post pictures of their food."

Dee turned to her, its gold-irised eyes unblinking. It unnerved Jessica seeing it appear almost human.

"Why would humans send pictures of food to other humans?" Dee inquired. Orvalus turned to Jessica, and coyly smiled, she knew he wanted an explanation as well. Poke focused in the direction of the drawer, nervously wringing his hands.

"Yeah I dunno really. They think they're sharing, but I think it's to make other people jealous."

"Those are… strange customs," Orvalus said.

"Can you let him focus, please?" Poke interrupted nervously, then Peek flashed in his temple. "Oh, right. Yeah. How do you feel in there…? You're serious?" Poke's shoulders dropped in relaxation.

After a moment the drawer opened back up and Poke rushed up to retrieve the smartphone. As he pressed the home button, a large, smiling, yellow emoji filled the screen. Peek flashed in Poke's temple and then gave the "thumbs up" on the screen. Jessica reached for it and Poke turned away from her, still clutching the phone, having a conversation in his head.

"Jessica, leave him alone. It will… be all right." Orvalus commented as Jessica reached for the device.

Jessica eyebrows arched and her lips downturned. "You don't understand, we always have our phones on us, it's like…"

"An extension of your brain?" Poke said into the air without turning around.

"Yeah."

The smartphone, controlled by Peek, flashed a sad emoji, then switched to the "hug" emoji. Poke's temple LEDs rippled.

"This is fun though, I like you this way," Poke spoke to the phone, and the emoji switched to an angry face. "Right, I'll give it back." He sighed, and then handed the phone back to Jessica. She, in turn, relaxed.

"We have a problem with these things, I admit," Jessica explained to Orvalus, who regarded the whole exchange with suspicious eyes.

"We experienced the same issues when we …approached The Singularity. Some of us could not cope with the new course of our existence. Remind me to tell you of the separatists sometime."

"Singularity? What has this to do with black holes?" Jessica's education demanded to be included in the conversation.

Orvalus laughed, deep and throaty, and even Dee smiled.

"The Singularity. The point in which we became part of the Hegemony. When our kind achieved sentience and made The People what we are today. *De novo* AI, emulants, and Takki living together." Dee explained, rotating its index finger to encompass the entire shop around them.

"Are there People who don't like this? You can't have complete agreement. That's not possible."

"Yes," Orvalus answered, "but that is a story for another day. We must return and prepare for Administrator Dux's arrival."

The lights in the room dimmed to the displays on the drawers and running lights toward the door. It felt suddenly quiet and peaceful to Jessica, despite the inescapable sterility of it all.

The three stepped out into the street again. Jessica immediately put her hood up and adjusted her sunglasses. They headed back to the ribbons and Orvalus let her pick the times to jump on and off of them. She slipped once or twice, using the excuse of, "I'm from Atlantis," even though she knew it was meaningless. Once out and in the part of the city she recognized, Orvalus and she got fruit from a nearby stand. It stood unoccupied, and people took what they needed and moved on. Jessica wondered if they still used money. As a matter of fact, she was not sure what drove their economies other than information sharing. She made a mental note to ask for an explanation when things settled down.

Peek flashed in Poke's temple, and buzzed from Jessica's pocket. Before she could check, Poke answered, "Dux is here, she's waiting for us."

Orvalus checked a clock at the side of the closest building. It read: 17:40.

"She's early?" Jessica exclaimed, not hiding her annoyance.

"The Administrator arrives when she sees fit," Dee responded, shepherding the group across the street. The street was now darkened in the shadow of the other buildings around it, maintenance robots scurried along the sidewalk, removing detritus and making repairs to the smallest of imperfections.

They turned the corner to see the tall, slender form of Administrator Dux standing in front of the familiar post-and-lintel frame of the Terran Gate. Above the door read the words: "Bellerophon Transportation #4: Terran Gate" and underneath a square and a circle. Jessica silently mouthed the words she understood, but could not figure out the shapes.

"What are those symbols?"

Dee explained, "The circle means gate transportation, the square denotes permission is needed."

"Permission needed to use the gate and store food?" Jessica wondered aloud.

"What do you mean?"

"When I first got here, the lintel had a square, a circle, and a triangle."

Dee nodded, "Correct. Well done, Terran. Of course, that is in another dimension." The corner of its mouth upturned into a smile. Jessica started at the sight, and told herself to be more accepting of its new form.

Across the street Administrator Dux stood at the door, her slender figure resplendent with an orange robe. It was capped with a purple hood that lay about her shoulders. She had earpieces in each ear and spoke into the air; on the arrival of the trio, she put them in her pocket. They greeted her and entered the long hallway Jessica had become so familiar with.

Administrator Dux walked into the library and pressed several contacts on the control panel. At the stroke of a key, all the amber lights in the room went dark.

Poke gasped and gripped the wall behind him. "I can't see. What happened? Where is Peek?" The anxiety in his voice steadily increased to near panic. The administrator threw a glance to Orvalus, who responded.

"It is fine, the Administrator has… disconnected us from the planetary network. Give it a moment to…"

As if on cue, the smartphone in Jessica's started vibrating. She pulled it out and read the screen, and the yellow emoji returned, with a smile and the words, "Receiving… Peek." She pressed the green phone icon and held it up.

"Hello?" she answered tentatively. Blaring static and electronic noises erupted into her ear so loudly she dropped the phone on the floor, wincing in pain.

Poke immediately relaxed and scanned the room as his temple LEDs flashed randomly. He apologized, picking the phone off the floor.

"Warn me next time, huh?" he said aloud, not hiding his frustration, until he saw the administrator's penetrating gaze fixed right on him. He dropped his gaze down to the phone and smiled.

"Before we send you on your way, you have to be disguised, you cannot possibly walk about on another world dressed as you currently are," Administrator Dux explained.

Dee stepped up to address the group. "I have assembled the patterns for appropriate Terran dress; we will don these outfits and walk amongst the Terrans without them even being aware we are in their midst."

Dee directed their attention to the large screen, on which the patterns for several articles of clothing displayed in perfect three dimensions. Two togas for the "males" and one stola for Jessica. Despite herself, she immediately laughed aloud.

"Is there a problem, Terran?" Dee inquired, its tone more questioning than sarcastic.

"Did you see me arrive in a toga?" She gestured down to her clothing, hoodie, sweats, and sneakers underneath an alien jumpsuit.

"No, you are not dressed in a toga. Those are for men."

"You're splitting hairs," she retorted, staring up at the bald pate of Orvalus. "We aren't dressing like that. What is it with you guys?"

A small smile drew across Administrator Dux's lips. "How do you suggest we disguise them?" she inquired.

Jessica thought for a moment, then spoke. "Well, when I was connected to The Teacher, you were able to read my mind, weren't you?"

"Yes," Dee responded, "we have all of the information archived." It stepped up to the control cabinet and called up a file; images from Jessica's mind filled the screen. A few more taps and images of Jessica in various states of dress appeared, displayed for everyone to see.

"WOAH!" Jessica ran up to the monitor, flashing her arms wildly and trying to obscure the view. The image paused with Jessica stepping out of a changing room and gazing into a mirror. She wore a blue and green bikini, with grey waves in a swooping topical pattern. Fifteen years old, sunburned, hair bleached a light amber, almost blonde. Her mother smiled on approvingly, her father attempted to avert his eyes by analyzing a price tag. She recalled how embarrassed she felt to have to shop with them instead of picking it up with Katelyn, but she forgot her suit at home during that visit to the beach at Cape May.

"I need to look at those in private, please," she implored.

"What? Why?" Administrator Dux turned to the screen and at the embarrassed frown on the young woman's face and then back at the woman standing before her, who wore the same frown.

"Oh, of course." She stepped up to the cabinet and pressed a few contacts. The monitors turned off, and one lit up from the top of the panel. A few inches on a side, it was small and allowed only Jessica to see the display.

"I'll find something."

After a moment she called back. "Here, these should be fine."

The administrator turned back to the cabinet and switched the view from the small monitor to the large one. Two images appeared on the screen, one of her father wearing jeans and a blue shirt, a grey sport coat over the top, brown shoes. Another image featured a young man from her class, with jeans, black hoodie, grey beanie, black sneakers. He sported a black pair of Wayfarers. A large backpack lay at his feet. Poke laughed when he saw his "disguise."

"Believe me, no one will pay any attention to you."

Dee studied the screen. "I am to wear this? I do not appear as young as the man in the other image."

"Again, no one will notice you. They will think you are our father or another person." Jessica reached under her jumpsuit and tugged at the hoodie. "I'm not exactly in a gingham dress here. Being underdressed will keep you from being noticed. Our culture has gotten a lot more informal since the last time you saw it."

"These are acceptable then?" Administrator Dux asked, about to press more contacts on the cabinet. Jessica nodded. A final button was pressed, and one of the alcoves in the library closed silently. An electric hum filled the air. She turned and addressed the group.

"As we know, KT does not allow unauthorized gate travel. This has been made so since the Time of the Trials and it has kept us safe. Although I agree with this policy, I feel it is limited here. KT is of a single mind, as designed, we are not. With notable exceptions."

Dee nodded at the recognition.

"However, it does present certain problems. How does one circumvent a device designed to keep us safe? Should we even do it at all? Is it wise to limit ourselves and never take a risk?"

Jessica arched her eyebrows and thought to herself, *She really is a politician.*

"In an effort to keep us safe, we have spent a great deal of time to make sure the system works. The best way to do so, is to both test it, and to have a control. A way to get past the safeguards without triggering those safeguards. Either we do it with code," she nodded to Poke and Peek, who flashed brilliantly, "or with something physical. A device. A contrivance. I happen to have one."

With much flourish of her elegant arms, the administrator reached into her pocket and produced a stone. Roughly the size of her doubled fists, it resembled a river rock. On Earth, anyway. Jessica instantly recognized it.

"A rock?" she asked, without waiting to be given leave to speak.

"Always impulsive," the administrator chided. Jessica did not avert her eyes in response.

The administrator continued, "This river rock is more than a mere stone. It is a Terran stone, from the foot of the Terran Gate."

Jessica jumped at the recognition, another piece of her home had sat there, all along.

"Administrator, I have never seen such a… device," Orvalus commented, leaning forward to get a closer look at the stone. It sparkled silver in the glow of the monitors.

"Of course you have not, only the current administrator of Bellerophon has access to the Silver Stone. We have kept it in our archives for thousands of years. As such," she gazed into the eyes of the assembled in turn, "you will not reveal your knowledge of this device to anyone. Is that understood?"

Dee's eyes briefly flashed blue, and Peek's LEDs similarly flashed blue in a following pattern. Poke nodded. Jessica glanced from alien to alien. *That wasn't a request*, she thought. She nodded along.

The administrator placed the stone on the control cabinet on a small space above an interface slot. "I have never used the stone myself, as I have not had a reason to until recently. This might take us a moment to get working properly."

She shifted the stone on the panel until it lay as flat as possible. The monitors switched from pictures of Jessica's life to those of Sol in an azure sky. The view drifted from an angle high in the sky, and floated closer and closer to the surface, with the boot of Italy coming into view.

Jessica's heart leapt for joy as a smile tore across her lips.

Chapter 20: The Terran Gate

"Is everyone ready?" Orvalus asked as he stood over the controls. All five monitors were on and showing the area around the library. The largest of the five, the one that dominated the entire wall, showed what appeared to be a pond of water, narrow and shallow. At the far end of the water where it met the land, the pool lapped crushed white stone, upon which grew thin grass. One side of the pond had marble stairs sloping away from the water, the other two ended in sharp walls three feet high.

"Where is this? It doesn't really look like Rome to me," Jessica commented, although she was afraid to admit out loud she had never visited Rome and only knew the Eternal City from pictures and the internet.

"This has always been the location of the Terran Gate. The city of Hierapolis," Administrator Dux answered.

"Hierapolis? That's in Turkey, not Italy."

"Why would they name a city after a bird? What is Italy?" inquired Dee. Jessica could still not get used to it even having a body, to say nothing of a face and a voice, however human it might appear.

"No, the country is Turkey, not the city. It's named after the Turks. Rome is, well in Italy now, but the city is the same." She desperately tried to recall everything she knew about the country. "It's… Asia Minor. Part of Rome. The Empire, not the city. An… Ana…Anatolia?"

"Yes," Dee answered, "southern Anatolia. A beautiful city, very civilized. I was introduced to the Civitatis Princeps during the reconstruction; a delightful man named Septimius Severus."

Jessica wrinkled her forehead and squinted. "Snape is named after an emperor?"

"Snape?"

"Never mind."

Orvalus picked up the Silver Stone and placed it into a depression on the control cabinet. It fit, but not to his satisfaction. He took it out, rotated it, and placed it back in. Again, it did not fit properly.

"Administrator?" he implored, showing the stone back to her.

"I don't know how it works, Gatekeeper."

"May I render assistance?" Dee reached for the stone. "This device is primitive." It turned the stone around in its hands, the frustration of not being able to interface with it directly became obvious. "Peek? Can you find this and analyze, please?"

The AI in Poke's temple flashed a brilliant amber, then flickered randomly. Poke looked up from the modified smartphone.

"It's in there, searching the museum archives for the information and that is encrypted." He paused and then spoke back to Peek, "No, we are not giving away our secrets. We work for the library. So, we only worry about the rules when you can get in trouble, but not me…? Why is that important? What do you mean we…" Poke pointed to his temple and wobbled his head to express his frustration.

"While you are there, should you need to travel secretly," Orvalus produced a small amber, gold, and green cube, three inches on a side, "you should be able to move around quietly with these."

Poke instantly grabbed the cube and stuffed it into his pack. "My favorite?"

"Yes, it is there. Try not to break it this time?"
Poke's gaze cast to the floor, even though he could not see it. Gazing at the floor, Poke continued relaying Peek's information. "It says to flip the stone to the long axis and press in. The depression should click. There is a command code it needs to put in on the cabinet. Uh, you'd better let me do that, the combination is big," Poke translated. He entered a sequence of numbers and characters, stretching on for a full minute and when the final sequence was entered, the gate flashed open — its electric blue glow filling the library.

Jessica reflexively jumped and dread filled her. Her hands shook. She could not tell if she felt excited to go back home or terrified at the possibility it would bounce her around the system again. It had been hard enough the first time, and now she had what could only be described as hostages. She stepped back from the gate and took a deep breath.

Orvalus, back at the control cabinet, read the data stream.

"The connection is stable, we're receiving data in both directions. There is no indication KT is … aware of us activating the gate. Peek, can you transmit into the gate and back? Your connection needs to be tested."

The face of Jessica's smartphone lit up. The screen read, "Calling… Home."

An amber light flashed on the control cabinet, and Orvalus pressed it. Immediately a cacophony of digital sound flooded the room, and the Takki and Terran covered their ears. Peek's LEDs flashed bright, and then dimmed, along with the sound.

Poke translated, "Sorry, there is a lot of noise in the gate. Peek didn't mean to scream."

Orvalus nodded and studied one of the display panels; in it the camera from the smartphone displayed in enormous resolution. In the other panel, lists of data poured forth.

Poke grabbed his pack and hoisted it onto his back. "We're ready," he said.

"I am ready as well," Dee said, stepping up to the gate barely an inch away.

"I'm ready too," said Jessica, swallowing hard. She stepped up behind Dee and Poke.

"Remember, you all need to come back together, or you do not come back at all," Administrator Dux explained, her face cold, as if she were admonishing a child.

"*We* will," Jessica responded.

"Have fun!" Orvalus interjected. "Take care of her."

Dee responded with a nod.

Jessica took one last look at the library and then stepped through. Her stomach lurched as she slipped the dimensions to Terra. The patch on the back of her neck throbbed and then went still. In a moment she heard the splash of water and felt warm air on her skin. Her eyes focused slowly, and briefly she felt as if she had gone blind. She was being led forward by a hand with cold fingers, and presumed it was Dee. As her senses slowly came back, she could hear

Poke splashing next to her, and the deliberate footsteps of Dee in front of her. She blinked her eyes, and the android came into focus. She breathed deeply and reveled at the smells of her homeworld. Something was different about the air though, and she could not quite place it. Lavender? She inhaled deeply through her nose again, looking around for the source of the fragrance. The dark sky lightened in the eastern horizon.

Dee beamed, and for the first time Jessica saw it enjoying itself, at least she thought it was.

It turned to her and smiled. "Welcome to Terra!"

Chapter 21: The Ploutonion

Jessica smiled back. Immediately her head began to swim, spots filled her eyes. She shook her head and scanned around her. The pool sat in the middle of what appeared to be a marble bathtub. The walls went up three feet on each side. She turned and saw a small doorway in the wall, barely the size of a person. It led to a cave where they had walked out of. The water in the bottom of the cave bubbled.

She shook her head again and her eyes tunnel-visioned, grey curtains pulled around the world. She heard yelling, panicked, terrified, and not human.

"Have to get out of here," she mumbled, "gate to Hell…"

In an instant Dee scooped her up and lifted her out of the pool, depositing her on the side of the bathtub. She could feel the warm night air blow across her face, and her eyes slowly began to clear.

"You are not in danger, relax. Your heartrate is quite high, and you are hyperventilating. You must regain control of yourself, or you will pass out."

"I'm okay, Dee, thanks," Jessica responded.

"No, not you, Terran."

Dee lifted Poke out of the water with one hand and deposited him next to Jessica. The lanky Takki writhed next to her, pawing at the LEDs on his temple.

"Peek! I can't see! PEEK!" he yelled.

"You must contain yourself, or someone will hear you," Dee chided, to no avail.

Jessica rolled over, shaking her head trying to clear it all the way. She grabbed Poke's hand and held it tight.

"Poke, I'm here, breathe," she said in soft tones, using the cadence that her father would when she was lost in a panic attack.

"Peek! Please!" Poke pleaded.

Jessica pulled the smartphone out of her pocket, and with the same hand tossed it to Dee, who caught it without moving its body save its arm.

"There is no power in this device," it explained quickly.

"Poke! Poke listen to me," Jessica said speaking to the alien in loud, clear tones. "Peek is out of power; we will charge the phone. It will be all right."

Poke nodded hesitantly.

"Peek has never gone offline before?" she asked.

"Only when it's trying to get its way. Is it dead? Please?" he implored.

Dee turned the phone over in his hand and examined the charge port. It held out the opposite hand, the first knuckle bent back, and a thin glowing cable extended from it, clicking into the port. "I can power the device; it may take a few minutes. Be calm, Librarian, the situation is in hand."

"Yes." Poke nodded again, emphatically this time. "Yes, friend Jessica, thank you."

Jessica helped Poke sit upright, brushing grass clippings off his back.

"Perfect place to put a gate," Jessica said, coughing and clearing her throat.

"The Ploutonion provides the Gate protection from inquiring minds. Only the priests worked here. We could move back and forth with impunity. The carbon dioxide levels are never high enough to harm human life. There must be a local temperature inversion, keeping the pool from clearing. Are you all right, Terran? How do you feel?"

Jessica surveyed the landscape, not answering the android. All around her stretched the ruins of the Roman city of Hierapolis, with low grass and Cyprus trees dotting the fields. The foundations of marble buildings were all around her. To her right in the distance, she could see the amphitheater, unmistakably perched on the side of the hill. To her left, buildings and columns, and farther behind, small modern buildings and lights.

In a moment, the smartphone came to life, with the smiling yellow emoji filling the screen. Peek's LEDs burst into light from Poke's temple. He sighed, and instantly relaxed.

Jessica took a breath and relaxed her shoulders.

"What time is it?" she asked, trying to get the pair to focus.

Poke responded, "Zero four twenty-one, local time. The Twenty-seventh of October."

"We'd better disguise you. Come on, stand up," Jessica said, offering the tall alien her hand and helping him up. She pressed the red button on her jumpsuit. It relaxed and fell off her body, revealing her sweatpants and hoodie.

Poke pulled off his pack and put it on the marble floor. He took Jessica's jumpsuit and stuffed it in, then pulled the clothes they made before leaving and distributed them to Dee and himself. Poke pulled the beanie over his eyes, covering Peek's LEDs in the process.

"I can't see," he called, anxiety rising in his voice again.

Jessica pulled the beanie back up, uncovering his eyes, the bottom of Peek's three LEDs exposed under the rim.

"Much better." Poke smiled. "Thank you again, friend Jessica."

"Can you guys see?"

"Yes, but not as clearly as I'd like. We will be… ok?" he asked, using the idiom.

She turned to the android. "How are you, Dee?"

Dee stood staring off into the distance, surveying the ruins around it. The android appeared perfectly modern in any respect: jeans, hoodie, blonde hair. Its gold-irised eyes were the only giveaway of its inhumanity. "I am fine. What happened? This was not how I last saw this city."

"A bunch of earthquakes. It wasn't burned or anything."

"Disappointing. I enjoyed that city. Still, I can tell by the street layout this is the same location."

"The sun will be up in a few hours, I think, so we need to get away from here."

Jessica stood as she thought of their situation. In all the rush to the Gate, she never considered how they would get from Hierapolis to New York without attracting attention. Or without having passports, plane tickets, or speaking Turkish for that matter. She watched as Poke and Dee put on sunglasses similar to the ones Orvalus gave her. In the dark of the night she felt unsure how they would be able to see, and then she realized neither of them physically saw what they were looking at. A plastic screen would not block them in any way.

Poke reached into his pack and pulled out a small grey patch, similar to the one Orvalus had put on her neck back in Bellerophon. He slapped the patch onto the back of his neck. Jessica reached back to hers.

"I don't need this anymore, right?"

Quickly Dee interjected and reached toward her. "No! Do not remove the vibration patch!"

Jessica jerked her hand down quickly. "Why? I don't need it, I'm home."

"Once the patch comes off, it will no longer function. Spare patches have been packed, but there are not many of them. Removing the patch will also leave you disoriented, and you will not have time to adjust. We must leave quickly for your home before we are noticed."

Poke reached into his bag and pulled out a band of elastic material and wrapped it around his arm. Then, taking the smartphone from Dee, he held it against the band. The band grew around the phone, appearing to merge with it. Poke checked it and smiled; the yellow happy emoji rolled around the display.

"So how do we get there?" Jessica asked Dee.

"Right here," Poke interjected, and Peek flashed excitedly. Poke took out the cube Orvalus had given him, and he rubbed it lightly on three sides with his finger. The cube glowed amber along the edges, and then broke open with a "click." It split along those lines into three pieces, identical in shape but different in color. He immediately put the amber one in his pocket, handed the green to Jessica, and the gold to Dee.

"What do we do with these?" she asked.

"You wanted to get to New York. This is how we do it."

She watched in amazement as the slice of cube began to unfold in one direction, flip over, and unfold in another. Like an origami crane, it kept unfolding and flipping over and over, until it fully expanded. Jessica's jaw dropped as Poke held out a pair of sleek metal wings.

Their ribs and feathers were made of the same material and shone with an amber hue. The metal felt lustrous and rich, as if carved from a single piece of the namesake stone. Along the length of the arms, amber lights ran and blinked softly.

Poke smiled and Peek flashed ecstatically.

"How…? How do we…?" Jessica stammered.

"Like this." Poke flipped the wings upside down and arched them over his back, like placing a backpack on from the front. She saw him shudder as the wings clipped on. He tested their function, retracting and unfurling one wing, then the other. With a final flap, he lifted off the ground and hovered before her.

"Magic wings," she gasped, gobsmacked.

"No, it is not magic, Terran," spoke Dee from behind her. She whirled around to see it similarly hovering. Its gold wings were an exact copy of Poke's, save for the color. "These are anti-gravity, controlled via an MMI. We fashioned them after eagle's wings so your prim… forgive me, ancient society would see us as gods and not question our abilities."

"Icarus was…?"

"A fool who did not understand how alien technology should have worked," Dee interjected quickly. "His father knew how use them properly, but the boy… boys make stupid mistakes. These are not meant to be taken out of the atmosphere. After that no Terran has been allowed to use them and Daedalus concerned himself with other things."

"He was Terran?" Jessica asked, turning the green slice over and over in her hands, which trembled at the thought of the wings use.

"He was. We hid ourselves better in the priesthood, and then decreed no technology should be shared with Terrans until they became more mature."

Dee folded up its wings and landed softly in front of her. "These work by connecting the nanowires to the spinal column of the wearer. They are not permanent, it should not hurt you, and we know they work perfectly well with Terran physiology. A child owned this pair last, therefore it should fit you properly."

Jessica breathed quickly. Although terrified, she had no reason not to trust it.

"You have to open it, so it will bond with you. Run your fingers along the sides like Poke did."

On cue, Poke streaked by overhead, laughing.

Jessica did as instructed and the wings unfolded in front of her. They shone like emeralds, with green lights running along the arms. Her heart raced and she swallowed hard. She flipped them over, and arched her hands over her head. "Like this?"

"Yes, Terran. When you put them on, you will feel a brief disorientation as your spine accepts this nanowire. It will burrow through your clothes, and attach almost instantly. There is no reason to fear."

She suddenly felt more nervous than before.

She nodded, and flipped the wings over onto her back. Instantly her body shook as it screamed to her that something foreign had entered her spine. Her muscles tensed and her breath held fast. She panicked, and attempted to pull the wings off her back, but they would not budge.

"Relax, Terran. They will come off when you are relaxed. Let it bind."

Jessica calmed her mind and slowed her breathing; the wings that had once felt like an invasion into her body felt like an extension of her arms. The more she relaxed the better she felt, as if the wings were coaching her along.

"You see? You can do it," Dee said to her, and smiled.

Poke soared overhead again, "Yay!" he exclaimed.

"Poke, I need you here," Dee demanded.

With a sigh, Poke landed and met the pair. "Right," he said without asking why he was needed and addressed Jessica. "You need to feel the wings and how they work. Think of it as trying to move your gallbladder away from your liver." Jessica raised a quizzical eyebrow, and Peek laughed. "Or that. Exactly like that."

Jessica closed her eyes and felt the wings. The right one unfurled and held straight. She felt herself tipping over in its direction, thought of the other, and it unfurled as well, compensating for the weight.

"Good, they should balance."

They did and Jessica shifted the weight on her back, relaxing both sides. She flapped them together, and could feel her feet becoming light. "This is amazing! How does it work?"

"I could tell you, but it's pretty advanced stuff. When we have time. Remember, there is fuzzy logic controlling the balance, but you are in control, no AI will help you. Don't let your emotions get the best of you. You don't want to end up like Icarus."

She nodded and Poke lifted himself back off the ground, smiling as he did so.

Jessica planted her feet firmly and looked up at the sky. "Here I go."

Chapter 22: On the Wings of Daedalus

Jessica imagined the wings, and how they should lift her; they slowly flapped faster and faster until she felt herself lifting from the ground. The feeling of lifting didn't come from the wings themselves, but rather from her feet, like she was being pushed from the bottom rather than pulled from the top. The disconnect was disorienting. Poke offered an explanation. "It's antigravity. The pack generates the field, and the wings move you, but it's propelled bottom up. You are doing well. Relax but not too much."

Jessica nodded and lifted herself higher, but still close enough to the ground to be safe, she thought. The wings flapped at a slow rate, and she marveled at the sound, the feeling of floating, and having no weight at all. Like her dreams where she could lift herself and float and upon waking wishing for it to be real. Here she hovered with her own pair of wings, staring at the horizon and its grey traces of dawn.

"Now, move toward me," Poke said, as he flapped backward, giving her space to meet him.

She envisioned moving forward, and she closed the distance by a few feet. She flew straight up and down however, more like hovering than flying. Poke tapped his forehead, reminding her to think. The fuzzy logic kept her level, but she controlled the motion. Poke moved back again, and Dee drifted down at his side.

Jessica leaned herself forward and concentrated on moving in that direction. The wings obliged and she steered toward the pair. The pitch left her facing the ground, and seeing her feet not touching the Earth terrified her. She clenched her eyes and dropped onto her face.

Poke laughed, and coughed to clear the tension. Peek flashed, laughing.

"One last thing," Poke said, landing beside her. "They can do this…" In an instant, he disappeared.

Jessica glanced up. "Holy… invisibility?"

"Yes. The antigravity field can also be moved and shaped. It's like having big invisible hands."

"That is so cool!"

"You can't fly and be invisible at the same time though. It takes too much power. It takes a lot of power to do anything really, so you have to be careful."

There was a hum to her left, and Jessica turned to see a few large pieces of marble lying on the ground. One by one they vibrated and then lifted in the air.

"You're doing that?"

"It takes concentration and…"

Upon lifting another piece, Poke became visible and dropped to his feet.

"When you hit the limit, everything shuts off," Poke said, his voice dropping in volume.

"Icarus?" Jessica asked.

"No, it was me. Orvalus was less than pleased when I broke my first pair. I was doing too much at once."

Ah there it is. I wonder if that's all.

"We must hurry, Terran, the sun will be up soon," Dee said as it drifted over her.

"Right." Jessica lifted herself off the ground, determined to get it right.

She lifted and floated toward Poke again, who continued to recede as she approached. She kept pace and moved toward him. Poke lifted higher and she followed. He receded faster and she followed. She wondered if this had been how she felt the day she suddenly stood and walked into her mother's arms.

Aiming for a cypress tree, she lifted higher and moved faster, angling herself in the horizontal to reduce drag on her body. In a moment she stood on the top branch, terrifying an owl who went screeching into the dawn, hooting incessantly.

"Perfect!" Dee exclaimed, "let's go."

The trio rose even higher and moved opposite the sun and the ground beneath them sped by, faster and faster. Dee and Poke kept pace with her, Poke in the front and Dee in the back. When Jessica dared relax enough to speak, she asked, "How high can we go? How fast?" A smile stretched across her lips.

Dee cautioned, "You cannot go more than a few hundred meters off the ground, and you cannot move more than eight hundred kilometers per hour. The wings do have shielding to keep you warm and allow you to breathe, but those are the limits of endurance for your biology."

Airplane speed, Jessica thought. "Can you go faster?" She leaned into the angle and sped up, seeing the grey outline of the Aegean appear on the horizon. Dotted small towns and farms came and went underneath.

"Yes, Terran, I can break the speed of sound on your world, and have done so on many occasions. But I will not be traveling so fast today."

She took another breath as she lifted higher, avoiding a radio tower.

"It's going to take us a while to get there. We're going to stop, right?"

Poke drifted back. "We'll need to eat and take bathroom breaks, but we did bring food."

Jessica flapped over to him and undid the strapping on the pack dangling off his feet. It moved at the same speed as he did and was not affected by the wind. Amazed she could maneuver the wings so expertly so quickly, she felt the temptation to pull herself up into the sky and touch the sun as well, but she learned from Icarus's lesson. She decided to do something less radical and got food, pulling out an apple.

"You know, I could really go for some tofu and rice."

"What is toe-fu?" Poke asked, as she handed an apple to him.

"It's your basic Chinese dish. My mom makes the best with the family recipe. I'll give you some when we get home."

Poke smiled. "I'd like that very much."

Dee sped up behind them. "We have a long way to go, focus on the journey ahead."

The trio stopped on the outskirts of Rome to take a break and find a place to go to the bathroom. Jessica found it difficult to show Poke how to go in the woods without being familiar with his anatomy. After she spent minutes using extensive euphemisms for body parts, Poke simply dropped his pants and walked behind a tree. Dee explained nanites removed waste directly from the bloodstream; they were removed in a cylinder on the hip. Here their nanites would not function, as they had no direct connection to the Hegemony.

Jessica desperately wished she could stop and explore the Eternal City. She had only traveled to China and Taiwan a few times in her life, but never made it to Europe. Not for lack of interest or tying - the occasion and timing never happened for her. When she finally made it, she couldn't stop, and spent her time teaching an extra-dimensional being to pee in the woods.

After resting under an olive tree and eating bread, Jessica managed to trade for the apples Poke brought, they lifted up again into the warm October Mediterranean sky. They flew quickly over the rest of the inland sea and accelerated over interior Spain and landed in the coastal town of Pontevedra. There they waited until noon, wanting to have the sun as high overhead as possible as they flew over the Atlantic. They took a siesta on the wooded island of Isla Tambo. Just after noon, they ate more, went to the bathroom again, and flew off toward the New World.

The endless expanse of the Atlantic stretched on before them; mile after mile of grey-blue water drifted by underneath. Jessica always hated flying in a plane over bodies of open water. She had a deep fear that if something happened, they would be lost at sea with no one to rescue them, and at the mercy of the open water. She silently prayed to herself, hoping nothing would happen along the way. Dee would, of course, do its best to make sure nothing would happen to them, and reassured them it would keep it that way. Under its care she was extended the honor of its primary directive, to never let any harm come to a sentient being, through action or inaction. Still, the six or so hours it took to cross the Atlantic proved to be the most anxiety-provoking of her life.

Then, as the sun set, the blinding lights of the city of New York came into view, and her heart leapt for joy. They maneuvered close to the water, coming right up the Narrows into the harbor, passing the Statue of Liberty and curving west, landing on the cool and rapidly darkening lawn of Liberty State Park in Jersey City.

Jessica surveyed the landscape around her, and breathed deeply. She was home. The skyline on the other side of the Hudson River shone brightly like a beacon welcoming her back to her reality. She dropped to her knees in the darkness and closed her eyes, her green wings falling off and retracting back into their cube slice.

"Are you… okay?" Poke asked her.

"I'm all right," she responded, standing up and pocketing the folded wings. "It's a little overwhelming."

Dee scanned the area, finding it completely unrecognizable.

"Welcome to Jersey City, New Jersey. United States of America. Earth," Jessica announced, ignoring the Latinized from.

"Terra." It corrected her, to which she smiled, having neither the strength nor will to argue.

Jessica pointed over to the Liberty Science Center on the north side of the park. "We can get the light-rail on the other side. Let's go, I'm hungry."

They walked to the train in the darkness, smelling the cold grass and hearing the leaves crunch as they went. As they turned the corner and met the lights of the train station, Jessica caught a glimpse of the ferry leaving the dock and returning to Manhattan. She didn't recognize it, even though she took them nearly every day.

Must be new.

Chapter 23: Jersey City

The trio stepped up to the kiosk to purchase tickets for the light-rail. The sparsely populated train provided relief in a smaller chance of anyone recognizing them, but in typical fashion of the Northeast, hardly a glance was given to them from the few people who were there.

Jessica pointed to the map above her, showing the stops they needed to make.

"So, we are at Liberty State Park, and we need to get to the West Side Avenue stop. So, four stops from here, and there are three of us so we need three tickets." She felt as if she were teaching "out of towners" how to use the system. She smiled when she realized the obviousness of that truth. Reflexively, she reached for her wallet in her pockets. They were empty.

"Great, I don't have any money. We can't pay to get on."

Dee and Poke scanned the kiosk.

"Money?" Poke asked.

"A primitive form of exchange, a step above bartering, where participants agree on a price for a service, and then pay with an agreed-upon medium," said Dee without prompting.

"Heh, I wouldn't say we agreed to the price," Jessica commented, pressing buttons to see if she could call up her account. The stations were unmanned, and the conductors on the train would need to see her ID before she could buy more tickets. She thought quickly: a mile to her house, not far, but after the long day, the prospect held little pleasure. The kiosk beeped behind her.

Poke held the smartphone against the card reader as its screen flashed randomly. Jessica shot a glance up at the LCD screen. It displayed gibberish and flickered.

"What are you doing?" she hissed.

Poke smiled at her. "Peek knows a way."

Jessica swiveled her head around checking for the security cameras. Sure enough, one pointed right at them. She jumped between the camera and the kiosk, obscuring Poke and Peek.

"Stand next to me," she whispered to Dee, who promptly stood beside her.

"So, you aren't all lawful good on an alien planet?" She asked Dee quickly, trying to appear nonchalant and coming off badly.

"It would not be wise to attract attention to us, Terran."

"Stealing is fine though? With a camera on us?"

"We are on an important mission, and we need to…"

Dee was interrupted with the sound of tickets printing and dropping out of the kiosk. Poke smiled and tapped the smartphone, and a large smiling emoji appeared on the screen.

Jessica quickly took the tickets out of the kiosk and stepped to the side of the track, motioning for the other two to follow her. "I swear, I'm home for ten minutes and I'm already breaking the law," she hissed again.

"Relax, Friend Jessica, *we got this*," Poke said calmly.

"We got this? When did you learn that?" Jessica demanded, her voice rising.

"We connected to your internet as soon as we arrived in Hierapolis," Dee explained.

"How do you think Peek knew the time?" Poke questioned rhetorically.

Jessica sighed and shook her head, "Barely on Earth, and you were already hacking."

Dee drew in a "breath" - although it was more for speech and not for oxygen - and began to remind her The Hegemony preferred the Latinized name, when the horn for the Bayonne-bound train sounded.

"Right, this is our train. Wait for the doors to open, it's not as fast as the ribbons."

With surprisingly minimal effort, the trio boarded the train and stood on the opposite side of the car, grasping the straps hanging from the ceiling.

"Do you wish to sit down?" Dee asked Jessica.

"No, someone might need them who can't stand up. I don't need them, I'm fine," Jessica said even though she was exhausted from the long day and her experience.

Her father had taken her on the train when she was little and showed her the ropes. The light-rail, the PATH, the subway, Amtrak. She had ridden all of the rails in the Northeast before she turned six.

"Who gets a seat on the train first sweetie?"

"Disabled people, old people, ladies, and little kids."

She gazed up at her father, eyes crossing with concentration. He leaned way down to kiss her on the head.

"That's right, baby."

She reached over with her free hand and wiped a tear from her eye; the strength of the memory had been overpowering.

The conductor came into the car, nodding hello to the passengers and checking all their tickets. Jessica nudged Dee and Poke, and bade them pay attention. With barely a nod, the conductor checked their tickets and moved on, adding a perfunctory, "Four stops."

Dee stared out of the window and surveyed the landscape around them. Not the prettiest section of Jersey City, and definitely not the prettiest of New Jersey in general; Jessica felt both ashamed and proud as she watched the android take in the sights. Poke and Peek were, as usual, engaged in their own conversation.

"Fascinating. How much your world has changed," Dee said as it switched to the windows facing Manhattan.

"Things change a lot. It's the way it is," Jessica explained, more philosophical than she wanted to be. She stared up at the edifice of One World Trade across the Hudson. "That building wasn't even here when I was born."

"Yes, September eleventh. A tragedy. Your culture endures much pain. So much of it self-inflicted."

"We do what we can," Jessica explained.

"You will learn you are not isolated, and your place in the larger multiverse will become apparent."

Jessica turned to it, their faces reflecting off the dark windows and the gleaming city beyond. She regarded it quizzically. Did it have emotions after all? Real emotions and not an approximation?

Minutes later the train drew up to their stop, and they alighted quickly. Dee and Poke made a point of waiting for everyone to leave the car before they did. Stepping out of the parking lot, Jessica spied her apartment building and the sandwich shop below. All she could think about was getting into her icebox and heating up her mother's food.

They waited for the stoplight at the corner to change. When it did, Jessica stepped into the street quickly to beat the cars out of the parking lot.

"Where are the terraces?" Jessica questioned as she scanned the facade of the apartment building while crossing the intersection. "How long was I gone?"

Dee, watching the stoplight with intense interest from the corner, answered without turning away. "According to our calculations, your arrival date is within plus or minus five days from when you left."

Jessica stopped dead in the middle of the intersection, blocking traffic coming out of the light-rail parking lot. She shook her head.

"Hey, baby! Move that ass!" yelled the driver of the lead car coming out of the lot.

Jessica turned slowly, her lips trembling, her eyes laser focused on the middle-aged man behind the wheel of an ancient Ares-K car. She raised the middle finger on her right hand, and grimaced angrily.

In a flash Dee took her in its arms, ran across the intersection, and deposited her on the corner in front of a sandwich shop. It turned to the car and waved, bowing its head in supplication.

"She crazy or somethin'?" The driver yelled as he pulled down the street, away from the pair. Poke had not yet left the other side of the intersection.

"You must be more careful, Terran. Had I not interceded…"

"Son of a bitch, who the hell does he think he is?" Jessica fumed from the corner, staring at the car until it turned another corner and disappeared.

Poke, having crossed the corner finally, stood erect at her sudden anger.

"Friend Jessica…," he said trying to distract her.

"Goddamn jerk, he's in the car, I have the right of way. Move my ass? Who the fu…"

"Jessica Chao!" Interjected Dee forcefully. The shock of using her name stopped her mid-word.

She quivered with rage, her face flushing pink. In a moment she blinked back tears, and shook her head. "Wow, I'm letting my crazy show here," she apologized while looking up at her building. *Where is the terrace? Am I seeing things? It's that patch… I hope.*

"That is fine. You are under a great deal of stress. Let us get you inside so you may collect your thoughts," Dee soothed.

"And be less obvious," Poke said, pointing to the customers in the shop, brazenly gawking.

Jessica took a breath and nodded, then headed toward the vestibule of the building Her apartment was above the sandwich shop. At least she thought it was. She opened the door and stepped inside, making sure the aliens were behind her. She instinctively felt in her pockets for her keys.

"Damn, my keys are upstairs, too. I can't get the elevator without them."

The smartphone flashed.

"Should we hack the system?" Poke translated.

Jessica turned to Poke, who held up the smartphone. A smiling yellow emoji filled the screen.

She smiled and shook her head. "No, there is a less high-tech way of doing things. We can take the stairs. I hope Katelyn is home."

Jessica stepped over to the call box and pressed the button for her apartment; it buzzed loudly. She took her finger off and waited, then she buzzed again.

"Hello?" came a voice from the speaker.

Jessica shook with joy at hearing her best friend again after what felt like a thousand years.

"Hey, Kate, it's me. I don't have my keys."

A pause for a moment, then a response.

"Me? M-Me who?"

"Katelyn, it's me, Jessica. I'm downstairs and forgot my keys."

"Jessica? … No, you're not."

Jessica stepped back and knotted her brows, pressing so hard on the call button her fingertip turned white.

"Kate? What the hell? It's me. You gonna buzz me up or what?"

"I'm coming down," Katelyn said quickly and then cut the line.

"What's going on?" Jessica said out loud, as the two aliens stood there, motionless.

Jessica turned around, gazing down at the floor and muttering to herself. In a moment the elevator door opened. Jessica smiled, tears coming to her eyes.

"When is your hair green…?" she asked and Katelyn immediately cut her off.

"Okay, stay where I can see all of you. The police are already on their way."

Dee focused on the pair, rapidly glancing back and forth; it took a half step forward and then stopped, looking around again.

"I said stay there!" Katelyn wedged her foot in the elevator door to keep it open and brandished a stun gun.

Jessica stepped right up in front of Katelyn. "Katelyn Finnerty, what the hell are you doing?"

Katelyn's hand quivered as she pressed the trigger on the stun gun. The blue arc jumped from pole to pole and filled the air with ozone. She thrust it in front of her, showing her intent to use it. Her eyes welled with tears.

"You're not Jessica!" she yelled.

"What?" Jessica shot back, glancing back and forth from Katelyn's green and red hair, and then at the stun gun, "How am I not?" she pleaded.

"Because…" Katelyn stammered, "…because Jessica's…dead!"

Chapter 24: Katelyn Finnerty

"What?" Jessica gasped. Her jaw stayed open after her final aspiration, her eyes went wide.

"Yeah, dead. A corpse. I was at her funeral."

Dee vibrated. "Tell her…" it started in, its voice small, "tell her something only you would know."

Poke quickly turned away to face the door, holding the smartphone up to the glass.

"I… I…" Jessica stammered, desperate to come up with anything that would prove her identity unequivocally, "Dumplings! You love my mom's dumplings! You always eat them before I do, so she keeps bringing them."

Katelyn's eyes narrowed. "That's all you got?"

Jessica sighed, her gaze darting to the floor. "Jamie. I introduced you to your boyfriend Jamie… you guys were about… damnit," she swore, remembering they had broken up in a dramatic, and very public, way.

Katelyn held up the stun gun. Dee's eyes flashed blue, and a tortured expression peeled across its face.

"This is NOT possible, who the hell are you? STOP LYING!" Katelyn screamed, attracting a glance from passersby outside the building.

Jessica started crying, and her hands shook. "I… you… you were the person who found me after I snapped after Dad died. You found me in Bayonne Park, about to throw myself into the bay. You talked me off the bridge and gave me your sweatshirt. You wrapped around me for an hour until we drove home. You let me cry all night."

Jessica's gaze again dropped to the floor, tears falling with a splash on the cold tile.

"You kept me alive. You convinced me not to kill myself and to re-take physics with you. You brought me home. We never told anyone. Ever."

Jessica stood there, holding herself up against her own desire to collapse from exhaustion. Tears streamed from her swollen eyes, and she trembled from head to toe.

Dee overcame its potentials and pivoted to keep Jessica from collapsing, but the sound of the stun gun hitting the tiles interrupted it. Katelyn slid up beside her, and wrapped her arms around Jessica. Dee stood back and watched them embrace.

Poke, still scanning out of the glass door reminded them, "What about 'the police?'"

Katelyn glanced up from the quietly sobbing Jessica, and stared at Poke, her eyebrows knitted together. She turned her head to listen better.

Dee responded to Poke in their native tongue, "She does not understand us. You did not learn English before we left Bellerophon." Peek flashed from the smartphone, its laughing pulse. Its LEDs flashed frantically in Poke's temple.

"Really? You want to do the talking? Try squeezing all your data out of the speaker. You'll sound like a baby," Poke cajoled aloud in Standard, unnerving Katelyn even more.

"Who the hell are you guys? Damnit!" Katelyn demanded, scanning the floor for the stun gun.

Peek jumped in from the smartphone using the voice of the digital assistant, speaking clear English. Its voice sounded tiny and childlike, indeterminant of gender. "Friends. Jessica brought."

Poke nodded and smiled sheepishly.

Katelyn held Jessica in her outstretched arms so she could see her face fully. "You have a lot to explain."

Peek, speaking for Poke this time in its newfound voice, reminded again, "Police?"

Katelyn gestured to the stun gun. "I didn't call them."

Jessica stumbled to the elevator as Katelyn grimaced at the two aliens and then followed her into the car. "Are you sure this is safe? I'm taking a big risk here."

"Yep, they saved my life."

After an uncomfortable elevator ride and a silent walk down the hall to the apartment, they stepped into Katelyn's place. Jessica immediately walked in and flopped down onto the couch, leaving the aliens to stand in the kitchen just inside the doorway.

From her position Jessica scanned the apartment, exactly as she remembered it, right down to the paint-flaked tin ceiling, but things were different. Decorations were missing, the wine glasses were in the wrong cabinet, and where there should be a door to their terrace, stood a floor-to-ceiling window with no access to the outside. Jessica leaned back, burying her head into the couch cushions and covering her eyes with her left hand.

"This isn't Earth, is it?" she asked into the air, but directed it at the two extra-dimensional occupants of the small apartment. Katelyn sat down next to Jessica and put her feet up on the coffee table.

"Let me guess," she commented, grinning at the two aliens, "you're from an alternate dimension."

Dee answered for all of them, "Technically speaking, young miss, we are all from another dimension, including Jessica. She is from a different dimension to ours as well."

Katelyn turned to Jessica, who smiled and gestured for Dee to continue.

For the next twenty minutes, Dee relayed their story of how Jessica happened to enter the gate, how Orvalus found her on the edge of oblivion, and the task the administrator set for them. Jessica took over the lecture once they arrived on this planet, and their journey here.

"But this isn't home for me, obviously," she remarked to Dee, with an accusatory tone.

"This is the address Administrator Dux provided to us. This is also the same Terra I have been to thirty-seven times in your history. This is exactly the place I expected."

"Then we bounced, again. KT screwed us." Jessica hissed. Katelyn's ears perked at the sound of the similar name.

"Administrator Dux provided the Silver Stone to circumvent the protection programs. This is not KT's doing," Dee explained.

"Great, screwed by a politician then, as usual."

Peek spoke from the smartphone. "Didn't know. No mad, please."

Poke took off his glasses, and Katelyn recoiled at the appearance of his solid green eyes. Peek responded, "We… come in peace."

Despite herself Jessica started laughing, a full laugh at the absurdity of the last few days. She was home yet wasn't. Dead and not. Nothing made sense. She decided it better to laugh at it and go with the flow instead of trying to stay ahead of the changes anymore. They all laughed, except Dee, who stood resolute.

After a moment, Jessica cleared her throat, "So, how did I… she die?"

Katelyn licked her lips and shook her head, "It's weird since you are here, but you… she caught COVID. You… she wasn't in a lot of pain, and passed in her sleep. I thought she overslept when I found her."

Jessica reached her hand out and grabbed Katelyn's shoulder, the way she always did when her best friend was upset.

"I'm sorry that must have been horrible for you," Jessica soothed. Katelyn nodded.

"How did you not catch the disease?" questioned Dee, breaking its silence.

"I didn't. I was exposed and tested positive, but I never got sick. They think Jessica got exposed…"

"At the restaurant," Jessica interrupted her.

"Yeah, but we couldn't be sure. Once it started spreading in October, it was already too late."

"October? It didn't start until January in my dimension." Jessica smiled to herself, taking pride in the way she expertly handled the situation at large.

"What happened to you?" Katelyn asked.

"I never caught it. Neither did Mom or Dad. We all made it out. You didn't get it either."

"Yeah, this is weird." Katelyn got up from the couch and went into the kitchen and poured more wine. "Do your friends…?" She gestured to the aliens who still stood between the kitchen and the living room proper.

"I do not require food or fluids," Dee responded.

Poke looked at the glass and nodded.

"Not much, connection will bad," Peek reminded him.

"That's wild," said Katelyn as she took out two more tall glasses.

"I didn't know it could talk, either," Jessica said.

When the glasses were filled and handed out, Katelyn sat back down on the couch next to Jessica, who instantly grabbed the peanut bowl from the coffee table, like she always did. She froze at the impropriety.

"Oh, sorry, this isn't mine," she apologized, retracting her hand quickly.

"Babe, your stuff is still in your room," Katelyn said, then sighed, "…her room. I doubt she'd have a problem with it."

Jessica smiled and grabbed a handful, popping them in her mouth.

"Geez, you're hungry."

Jessica stopped in mid-chew, her eyes growing wide.

"Yeah, Mom left some in the fridge yesterday, go for it." Katelyn said, referring to Jessica's mother.

Jessica shot off the couch and headed for the icebox. She hastily pulled open the door and reached in for the glass bowl her mother used to carry dumplings over to their apartment. Without hesitating, she threw them into the microwave.

"Sit down, guys." Katelyn gestured to the aliens as she stood up to join Jessica in the kitchen. They did, Dee sitting properly with good posture on a plastic lawn chair, Poke flopping into an oversized armchair.

"Her mom keeps bringing them over to me, I think she can't let you go. Wait…"

"I thought that too. Do you think we should tell her at all?" Jessica asked, already knowing the answer.

"Dunno, imagine how upset she would be if we show up with her dead daughter. What if you have to disappear again? Let's get this other stuff all sorted first, huh? We can talk about that later."

A soft knock rattled the apartment door, and then it opened slowly, everyone but Katelyn turned to the door surprised.

"Talk about what, Kate?" the male voice asked as he stepped into the room.

Jessica dropped the chopsticks she had gotten out of the drawer. They scattered across the floor, like icicles strewn across a frozen pond.

"DAD?"

Chapter 25: Ellwood Muller

Jessica stood behind the counter, her hands shaking, and her face contorting in confusion. Likewise, her father - at least the father from this dimension - leaned immediately against the door as it closed behind him, his legs slowly losing support of his body.

"Button?" He used the same pet name her father did on Earth. "No, that can't be you." His face flushed red and tears filled his eyes. His gaze darted back and forth between Jessica and Katelyn, demanding an explanation. Jessica knew him as one of the most articulate people she had ever known, and to see him completely speechless left her more concerned than anything. She tore around the counter and flung herself at him, sobbing as she ran.

"Dad!" Jessica croaked out between sobs. She knew deep down this was her double's father, no more related to her than a stranger walking down Fifth Avenue. Yet he smelled like her dad, she felt the same way in his arms. The crook of his elbows, the way his hands clasped behind her shoulder blades. Even his breathing was exactly how she remembered it. The conflicting thoughts slammed and danced in her brain. She ignored her rationale telling her to back away and stop embarrassing herself. She wanted to give this stranger some space. The more her mind tried to push her away, the more her body pulled in tighter.

"Someone explain this! Who are you?" His voice quavered and the words caught in his throat.

"It's me. Jessica. I know, I'm supposed to be dead."

She allowed reason to prevail and pushed herself out of his arms, one of the most difficult things she had ever done.

He looked down at her and instantly produced a handkerchief to wipe the snot from her face.

"It's okay, Ellwood," Katelyn reassured. "It's her. We have a lot to explain."

"Ellwood?" Jessica swallowed and wiped her face with his handkerchief.

"That's my name. Who are they?" Ellwood asked, gesturing to the aliens who had gotten up and now stood in the back of the room, respectfully keeping their distance.

Jessica tried to straighten up, hoping to bring some seriousness to her appearance. She tried to not look like the crazy person she felt like. How would she explain this to him and let him know that she was real? Her mind raced for things that only he would know. She'd have to tell him, and yet didn't want to reveal personal information in front of her new friends. Obviously, Ellwood knew everything about her, and to prove it, she'd have to go for the intimate details.

Too afraid to break the space and lose the emotional connection, Jessica leaned back against the counter. Katelyn rubbed the small of her back and handed her a glass of water. "Breathe, go slow," she counseled, and waited for Jessica to take a sip.

"Kate? You're in on this?"

Jessica finished her sip and handed the glass back to her best friend; nodding a thank you.

"Dad, what did I used to teach when you took me to your class?"

Ellwood's eyes narrowed. "Einstein–Rosen bridges, wormholes. Anyone would know that, Jessica taught eight years of it."

They were referring to when Jessica would warm up the class before his lecture. He taught environmental science at Hudson County Community College. From a young age she mimicked him as he taught, until one day he let her take the reins before class started. Nervous at first, she never looked back from that point. She'd never felt anxious or unsure of herself when she was "teaching." It was one of the few places she was comfortable. Her parents actively encouraged it so she would find a love of learning and accept going to college as an inevitability and not a choice.

"I know," she responded, "it's not when but what. Wormholes are real, I came here by one." Jessica surprised herself by her directness; she didn't feel the panic she had when explaining it to Katelyn. She knew if Ellwood were anything like her father, he would hear her out. He also wasn't holding a stun gun.

"You're from an alternate dimension?" he questioned, his wrinkled brow and smirk giving every indication he didn't believe her.

"You said they didn't violate the laws of physics. You encouraged me to explore it. That's why I went to NYU."

"But, that's all theoretical. No one knows if they exist."

Jessica knew she had to go deep.

"Remember that time on the train, coming back from the hospital when mom was really sick? We were the only ones in the car and I was really upset. You told me to breathe and not blame myself. I didn't make her sick from messing up the dumpling recipe. She already had an issue and it was just coincidence. You said, 'things in the world can be random, and it doesn't make sense. But never forget that we love you and it isn't random. I'll love you…'"

"…no matter where you are or how far away, even when I'm dead,'" Ellwood finished her sentence.

Ellwood relaxed, and slowly slid down the door until he was sitting on the floor. He dropped his hands on his knees and took a deep breath. After a moment he looked back up at her.

"Well then, what is the other thing you aren't telling me, why were you so surprised to see me?"

"You're dead honey," Katelyn interjected, exactly like the line from *The Terminator.* The accuracy of the guess made Jessica instantly flush. She teared up, and buried her face in her elbow.

"I'm dead?" he asked, slowly getting up from the floor, his knees creaking.

"Well, in my dimension… you are. You died a few years ago." Jessica blurted it out and stared at the floor, not wanting to give it more weight.

"COVID?" he asked, then caught himself. "You know, I don't want to know."

"What's your middle name?" Jessica asked as he walked over to her.

"Gerard, you know that."

"Not in my dimension, Ellwood is your middle name in mine," Jessica responded.

Ellwood laughed as he got himself a glass of water from the sink. "Let me guess, you are exclusively a tea drinker too?" He didn't even bother looking for any coffee.

"How many times did we go over that?" Jessica answered, with a chuckle from Katelyn.

"Dad, it's tree-bark. There's a place downstairs," he answered in a high falsetto, his mocking impression of nearly every woman he held close in his heart; Jessica's father on Earth did the same.

"Heyy… not cool," Katelyn responded.

Jessica was amazed at how well he was taking all of this. She felt the same about herself. Maybe it was shock, or the realization that he really was the same person no matter what dimension they were in and it mapped directly into her brain. This person could not be her father, but it felt the same. If he was cool with it, which he appeared to be, then she was too. Besides, how often does someone get the chance to see a dead relative come back to life? No zombies here; he was very much alive.

"So, then if I really am your father, then I have to do my job and find out who these two gentlemen are with you. They are from the other dimension as well?"

Ellwood put his glass in the sink and walked over to Dee, who slowly turned to address him. "Greetings Ellwood Chao, I am D417a, Liaison to KT, Overseer of the Terran Gate—"

"Last name isn't Chao." Ellwood interrupted it. "That's her mom's name." Jessica could instantly see he was putting the android on the spot.

"Forgive me," Dee said bowing. "I did not realize that you and her mother were unmarried."

Ellwood stopped and leaned in, narrowing his eyes.

"Are you calling my daughter a bastard?" he growled.

"I… do not… I…" Dee shook slightly as it attempted to fight off its confusion.

Ellwood laughed and slapped Dee on the shoulder, a thump emanating from the hit.

"Let me guess, you're an android, aren't you?" Ellwood surmised as he squeezed the metal and wires, a wide smile on his face.

"That is very astute of you Mr.…," It paused.

"It's Muller. Don't fry your circuits."

"Very astute of you, Mr. Muller. You need not worry, I cannot 'fry' a circuit, but my pathways can shut off."

"Are you… sentient?"

"Yes, Mr. Muller, I am as aware of myself and my place in the universe as you are."

Ellwood nodded, looking over Dee's face.

"Personal pronoun?" he asked, standing back and holding both of Dee's shoulders like he was sizing him up to wear a tuxedo.

"We often do not use pronouns, and directly use our names. However, to facilitate conversation, I use the pronoun 'it.'"

"You don't use contractions, do you?" Ellwood attempted to rock Dee from the torso. The android did not move.

"I do not, sir. Although it is possible for me, I… don't… like doing so. It seems inaccurate and misleading."
Ellwood smiled. "And whom do we have here?" He turned to Poke.

"Hello, sir." Poke straightened as he spoke. Ellwood lifted his gaze to meet him eye to eye when his tall frame finally stopped rising. Poke was still wearing his sunglasses, which hid his solid green eyes. He spoke in Standard, coming across in grunts and barks. Ellwood didn't flinch. Peek translated from the phone on the table using a masculine voice, not the one of the digital assistant.

"There is someone else in here? Hello." Elwood spun and picked up the phone, holding it in front of his face. "This is Jessica's phone. How did you get in there?"

"Big story," Peek responded. "I speak for Poke. He does not speak English yet. Does not like Teacher."

Ellwood smiled and put Peek down, then turned back to Poke.

"You're an alien aren't you, son?" Ellwood jumped right in. Jessica hated when her father disregarded social norms and went right for direct questions. She always bristled when he did so, as if he didn't really care how others felt about him.

"I am, sir. Your world doesn't exist in our dimension, so technically you…" Peek translated.

"I'm the alien! That's great, I've always felt different." Ellwood winked. "You eat meat? Veg? What's behind the shades?"

"Shades?" Poke inquired through Peek, looking around for help. Katelyn tapped her temple.

"Ah yes, shades. Friend Jessica felt it was better to hide my eyes. She was right, I'd be too obvious." Poke took off the sunglasses and did his best to smile for Ellwood.

"Cool!" Ellwood leaned in. "No sclera? No pupils?"

"No, we don't have those in our species, but I don't need them anyway."

"Why not?"

"Poke blind," Peek explained.

Elwood nodded and stepped back. He took out his cellphone and addressed Jessica. "I'm gonna text your mom…" His eyes immediately downcast. The reality came flashing back.

"Well, her mom. I need to let her know where I am. I have a feeling that this is going to take a while."

Katelyn stepped up and took the phone from his hand. "I'll talk to her."

"Kate, don't!" Jessica interjected, reaching for the phone.

"Babe, don't worry, that will kill her. I'm just gonna shoot the shit."

Jessica took a breath and stepped back. "Let her know I love her somehow?"

Katelyn nodded and disappeared into her room with the phone.

"You don't have anything private there, do you?" Jessica asked Ellwood, gesturing to the smartphone.

"Right, like I have a life or something," he said sardonically and then waved dismissively.

"I tell you what, let's order some food and sort all of this out. There has to be a reason why you are here other than to give me a heart attack. I need to know everything. Let's start at the top."

Ellwood plopped down on the couch, and Jessica came up and sat beside him.

Chapter 26: How Do You Judge a Culture?

"So, I sent you to NYU, only to have you skip out on us and disappear into a portal in your basement? This is how you repay me?" Ellwood joked, a smirk on his lips bunching his beard into the upper right corner.

Jessica cleared her throat and took another sip of tea, "You always said I should take the red pill."

"You weren't running from us, were you?" he asked, a more serious tone in his voice.

"Dad, really?" She paused after calling this man her father, feeling as if she was somehow dishonoring her real father. "I'm sorry, you're still right there in my head. My dad even had the same beard occasionally."

Ellwood nodded. "And you are still in mine. We need to figure something out, though, or it's going to kill the both of us." He stared into his coffee cup, the one his Jessica had given to him years ago. A black mug with the outline of Darth Vader, white on black, the words beneath, "Who's your Daddy?" He would take it to the coffee shop downstairs for half-priced refills.

"You can call me Ellwood since it obviously wasn't your father's name. I'm just gonna call you 'Button,'" he stated, without asking for permission.

"Sticking with the pet names?" Jessica asked, putting the teacup down and glancing over to the aliens who were sitting in the dining room talking to Katelyn. Poke's head was buried in a pizza box.

Ellwood laughed. "Why not? What are your friends searching for?"

Jessica pointed over to Dee, who stood at the reference to it.

"Administrator Dux wants us to be able to prove to her that this planet has progressed beyond the primitive barbarism of your past. Is your civilization worthy of connecting to the Hegemony, and can we trust you with the knowledge of the multiverse? There is risk of tearing the fabric of the universe, and we want to be sure that the chance is worth it."

"That's not very logical, son. What if it does break?"

Dee stood still for a moment. Its eyes flashed blue then slowly reverted to gold. "You are the only sentient species we are aware of in the multiverse. Is it not worth it to make the connection than be alone?"

Katelyn raised her right eyebrow.

Ellwood shook his head. "I don't think you are going to find it, then. This planet is pretty messed up sometimes. Sure, we have progressed a lot in the last couple of hundred years, but there is nothing terra-shattering about what we have achieved."

Jessica bristled at the use of Terra instead of Earth, it reinforced in her mind she was an alien on this world, too.

Katelyn interjected, "How dare you judge an entire culture, and then hold people hostage to prove your theory!"

"Hypothesis, young miss," Dee responded. "My companions and I are aware of the ramifications of this assignment. If there is no compelling evidence this culture is worth reestablishing contact with, we will not be able to return either."

Jessica thought about that for a moment. If they couldn't convince Administrator Dux —and by extension KT— that this society was worth connecting to, none of them got to go home. The aliens would be trapped on a world none of them belonged to. Or worse, KT could decide to drop them from existence when they tried to reconnect. The thought unsettled her, and her anxiety played havoc. A crushing feeling started in her legs, and simultaneously squeezed into her lungs.

"I can't let you guys die. I'd have to find a way to make sure you would at least get home. What about your thing about not hurting anyone in the Hegemony?"

"That is superseded when the safety of The People is at stake. We would be expendable in that case."

"The needs of the many…" Ellwood remarked.

"I won't do it then, I won't be a party to marooning you here for eternity."

Dee regarded Jessica as she sat there. "Do not despair, Terran, we will find a way. We are adaptable, and would not consider this as the prison you are implying."

That was hope! It is different based on its body!

Ellwood reached out and held her hand. "You're always home here." He smiled earnestly.

"First things first, then," Jessica delineated, standing up and addressing the apartment. "You have to stop calling me Terran. I'm not. They are." She pointed to Katelyn and Ellwood. "I never liked 'earthling' or 'earther.'" Jessica scowled, resolute in her thoughts.

"Fine then, what shall we call you?" inquired Dee.

"Um, Jessica?" Katelyn asked, rising to her feet.

Poke glanced at the group, and he stood too, "Friend?" he questioned, preferring his form of address.

"That's not what I mean. My… oh hell, whatever the word, that's what I want." Jessica smiled. "Gaian. There. Even though it doesn't fit. I'll use the Greek name."

"Demonym is the word you want. What happens if you ever run into another 'Gaian?'" Ellwood asked, eyebrow raised.

Jessica shook her head, exasperated and frustrated. "I dunno. She'll have to change her name."

Ellwood smirked and nodded. He gestured with his head to point to Terran Jessica's bedroom. "She was never that forceful."

"Second, we need to stop comparing everyone to everyone else." Jessica glanced at the ceiling and shook her head again, then continued. "We're gonna go nuts trying to keep it all straight. Third, we need to figure out how Dee and Peek can get the data they need without us giving ourselves away, and looking stupid at the same time."

"Oh, I'm not afraid of that," Katelyn interjected, taking another sip of wine.

"Knew you'd say that," Jessica said; a smirk flashed on her face. "I'm not sure how we are going to do it, though."

Ellwood finally stood up from the couch, groaning as he went. "Look out the window," he pointed to the picture window without a terrace, and then at the Manhattan skyline beyond. "This is the biggest city in North America. All we need is right there. Somewhere. The question is, where do we start?"

All eyes immediately turned toward Katelyn.

"What? Why are you all looking at me?"

"Are you serious? You're the social butterfly here. You know everybody and are the least introverted of all of us," Ellwood answered with complete incredulity. Katelyn smiled sheepishly.

Jessica suppressed a yawn. "What day is it, anyway?"

"Thursday, the twenty-eighth." Katelyn responded.

Jessica jumped up. "Halloween is soon! Perfect!"

"It is?" asked Poke, translated via Peek.

"Yeah! We can totally take you guys out without disguises!" Replied Katelyn as she walked over to Poke, shorter by a foot; she had to crane her neck to see up to his face. She broke his personal space, and Poke stepped back tentatively. Peek switched to the yellow embarrassed emoji.

"I think he's blushing," Ellwood whispered to Jessica, who stood smiling with her hands clasped in front of her, barely containing herself.

Katelyn smiled and backed away, looking around the small apartment. "You boys are going to have to sleep somewhere for a while I guess."

"I do not require sleep," Dee said quickly. "It is just as easy for me to stand."

"I can get the… couch?" Poke asked, gesturing to the long cushion. Katelyn nodded.

"I'll take Jessica's room," Jessica commented.

"And I need to get home," added Ellwood, taking a glance at his watch. "Ai Li is going to…" His cellphone and watch beeped.

"That's Mom," Jessica said.

After typing out a quick text, Ellwood said, "I will be here tomorrow at nine." He stepped over to Jessica, "Okay, Button, Jessica would have liked you."

"Likewise, Ellwood." She felt funny using the name. "See you in the morning."

"Later folks!" He waved goodbye to the room, and walked out of the door, locking it behind him.

Jessica stared at the door for several seconds after he left, still unsure if this whole experience was real.

She turned back to the group, feeling all the exhaustion, mental and physical, of the past few days weigh on her with unbelievable gravity.

"I'm going to get to bed. We should all try to get some sleep."

Chapter 27: The Familiar Yet Alien Room

After saying her good nights, Jessica walked into "her" room. She stood in the doorway for a few minutes, not quite sure of what to make of all of it. There were several get-well cards on her dresser, and empty flower vases.

She examined the room, trying to find a picture of what her Terran counterpart looked like, but could not find any. She presumed her mother had scoured the area and took any reminders with her. Knowing her mom, they were in a box somewhere in her house on Jersey Avenue, the one her "father" Ellwood had just left for.

Jessica sat down on the bed, which was covered in the blue spread her grandmother had knitted for her when she was a little girl. She pulled a section to her face and inhaled deeply, remembering her grandmother knitting this blanket during breaks while she labored away at the stove making dumplings. The same recipe she would teach her mother, and the one Jessica still did not know.

She lay back on the bed, staring at the popcorn ceiling; it appeared the same as well. In fact, the room looked exactly like what she was used to on Earth, without much of any difference.

"How can we be *exactly* the same?" she spoke aloud. "There has to be some difference?"

Getting up and moving over to the dresser, Jessica slid the drawer open, expecting to find something different. There was nothing shocking and revelatory about it. There were clothes in different locations than she would normally put, but they were the same clothes. As if she had put her laundry away, and forgotten how she stored it. She rifled through the drawer, searching for clean clothes to wear. She grabbed underwear, another pair of sweatpants, and an overly large sweatshirt she'd gotten from her father.

Stepping out into the hallway, she checked for the presence of the males in the apartment. Seeing none, she padded into the only bathroom, closed the door, and took a shower.

She stood under the warm water spilling down into the claw-foot tub. Turning, she let it drum on the back of her neck, and closed her eyes. Motionless for minutes, she realized how crazy the last twenty-four hours had been for her. It felt like a lifetime, or several as the case might be. Jumping from dimension to dimension, meeting actual aliens, and becoming one herself.

Amazed at her own ability, Jessica smiled and turned so the water ran down her face.

"You did it. You did all of that on your own." She thought about the woman endemic to this dimension. "You got through it without dying, but she didn't." Jessica felt a flash of anxiety clawing its way into her spine, trying to steal her accomplishments from her, yet again.

"No, I'm not going to let you take this away from me. You're not taking this away. Get back into your hole."

Although the anxiety didn't abate, she could feel it loosen its grasp as it clawed for supremacy. Jessica smiled and celebrated the small victory.

For the first time in a long time, she found herself enjoying the struggle. To lead her life without the fear she carried with her all the time. She vowed whatever happened to her in the future, she would face it without fear, and even if it did scare her, she would not stop. She would never give in, and she would eventually conquer it, no matter how long it took. Terran Jessica had run out of time to conquer her demons; Earth Jessica would not squander this chance.

"You gonna be in there forever?" Jessica heard Katelyn call over the water and from behind the bathroom door.

"Yeah, sorry, it's been a while."

"I can tell!" Katelyn yelled back and Jessica smiled.

Her hair might be different, but this version wasn't much different than hers. She had the same brassy attitude she remembered from when they were children. The same devil-may-care style, despite losing her best friend.

She turned off the water, toweled off, and got dressed in the other Jessica's clothes. At first, it felt weird to her. Her mouth drew into a thin line as she slipped on the underwear and sweatpants.

I hope these are clean. She laughed and put on the sweatshirt.

Jessica gazed into the mirror, surveying her own face. Her eyes were still puffy from the crying when Ellwood showed up. She felt better than she had in days, but also exhausted. She left the bathroom, crossed the hallway, and went back into the bedroom.

She hopped into the bed and smiled at the fact the mattress was squishy in the spots she liked. At that point she resolved to stop making comparisons. She had no idea how long she would be here until Dee and Poke found the information they were searching for, and spending the whole time drawing comparisons would drive her mad.

She shut the end table light off and closed her eyes. Drawing a deep breath, she felt her body slowly beginning to relax, the anxiety slipping away. Despite all she had been through, all the ups and downs, exhaustion won, and she fell promptly into a deep and restful sleep.

Chapter 28: A Walk in The Park

"Eww, are you serious?" Jessica stared at Katelyn with disapproving eyes.

"It's a hot dog, geez, you gonna go all vegan on me again?" Katelyn responded, putting a big line of spicy brown mustard down the length of the frank.

Jessica similarly poured mustard onto her pretzel, and shook her head. "Do you have any idea what is in those things? It's everything left over after they slaughter the animal. How can you eat that?"

"Like this." Katelyn slowly aimed the hotdog at her mouth, and bit off a full third of the sausage, adding "Mmmm," as she did.

The five were standing in Central Park on the south side of The Lake overlooking Bow Bridge. They were three hours into their tour of Manhattan.

"I think our friends," Katelyn said with a mouthful of food, and gesturing to the resident aliens, "need to see how we, as a culture, eat."

Dee stood back and regarded the scene. "This speaks volumes of your culture. You corral animals in pens, essentially torturing them, to grind them up and then shove them into their own intestines for your consumption. Yes, it shows me clearly."

Jessica grimaced, realizing this would be one more nail in the coffin of the barbarous Terrans.

"Look," Katelyn said as she scanned Dee up and down, "we can't pretend none of this exists. Does this make us any better if we have to cheat and not let you see this? We eat meat. Well, not all of us." She regarded the hot dog before taking another bite. "And this meat is good!"

Jessica curled her lips, took another bite of pretzel.

"What does it… taste like, Friend Katelyn?" asked Poke from the smartphone as he licked his lips, his blue tongue traced over them slowly.

"You cannot eat it!" Dee commanded, "I forbid you!"

"Not the boss," Peek said.

Katelyn responded by holding out the last third of the hot dog for Poke to take. Poke took the food from Katelyn's hand. He sniffed it first, then held it up to the phone so Peek could scan it. It added the camera click sound, and showed the eating emoji. He held it back up to his mouth, and then took a nibble.

"It's salty," he said, "and springy, like a fungus." He chewed, and glanced up, as if gathering his thoughts. "Also greasy. With decided aftertaste."

"Yeah, it's what we call the 'mystery ingredient,'" Katelyn explained, a mischievous smile on her face.

"I do like this. May I have my own?"

"Oh, you so can my friend. Come, let me help you." Katelyn took Poke by the arm and led him back to the hotdog cart parked next to a black Econoline van.

"Don't get him sick!" Jessica commanded as they walked away.

Katelyn waved her off.

"Your species still consumes others of your planet. Why?" Dee inquired after the two had fallen out of sight.

"It's about protein. We used to eat vegetables and then would eat meat when we could find it. Meat has been 'prestige food' since farming began, I guess."

Jessica surveyed The Lake, and marveled at the leaves in full turn surrounding it. Boaters dodged each other, and geese flew in and landed on the placid surface. There was hardly a cloud in the azure sky. Jessica turned to the sun, and closed her eyes. "Study after study has shown eating meat in large quantities is bad for you," she continued her recitation. "It's all processed, filled with chemicals, and not cooked like when we hunted it."

Dee regarded the people walking down the path toward the bridge. "If you could eat meat without processing it, naturally the way your ancestors did, would you?" Dee inquired of Jessica as she polished off the last bite of the pretzel.

"I've eaten plenty of sustainable meat in the past. I don't have an issue with it like other vegans do." She glanced down at her feet, watching the water lap at the shore just beyond them. "Everything dies. Everything feels pain. The only way out is eating fruits and seeds. But we don't need to keep doing this the way we do, it's bad for the planet. I don't eat meat to stop adding to the problems it causes."

"An enlightened point of view, Gaian," Dee commended.

"No, it isn't," Jessica said, turning toward the android. "Enlightened would be not giving my friends a hard time about it."

"You hold two conflicting thoughts simultaneously."

"Welcome to being human." She smiled.

Katelyn and Poke came back over to them; Poke held two hot dogs in one hand, and Katelyn held two cans of soda in hers, a bottle of water in her pocket. On her arm, she also held two more pretzels.

Jessica barely acknowledged the haul and sighed when Poke took a bite of a hot dog covered in relish, hot sauce, and grilled onions.

"He has falafel. I could get you some. I got another pretzel for you," Katelyn said.

"No, that's cool, I'm not hungry anymore. Besides, I …"

"Hey, I'll take it if you don't want it," interrupted a homeless man who had been following the pair back from the food cart. Jessica recoiled suddenly from the interjection. She cast her gaze to the ground.

"Here you can have this, I don't think she wants it," Katelyn offered, breaking the large pretzel and handing it to the man. "Wow, dude, you stink."

"Yeah sorry," the man said, pulling his beaten army surplus jacket up closer over his shoulders. His scraggly beard spilled from the open collar. "They close the bathrooms when it starts gettin' cold. I can't get in there."

"How long you been on the streets?" Katelyn offered him the water. Jessica stepped back against a nearby tree.

"Dunno, since…" He gazed up at the sky, his eyes matching the color. "Yeah, since Obama was president."

Dee regarded the conversation, its gaze darted back and forth between the two, and its fist clenched slowly.

"A long time, what happened?" Katelyn turned her body to face the homeless man but kept a respectable distance.

"Nah, man, I just didn't want to live under the man anymore, ya know? All that stupid shit we have to do all the time, and be good and all. What a waste of fu…" He stood back and took a bite of the pretzel. "Hey, sorry." He said covering his mouth with his water bottle.

Katelyn barely acknowledged it. "All good. You have a place to sleep?"

"Yeah, it's cool, a bunch of us are over at the Pond, got a little camp behind the concession stand. The cops don't hassle us till we get too big."

"What's your name?" she asked, handing him the other half of the pretzel. Poke, who had been watching and eating the whole time, finished off the second wiener, this one covered in ketchup.

"Jason," the man answered, an audible whistle came with the 's' sound. Undoubtedly created by the several missing teeth in his smile. "You are?"

"Katelyn. It's nice to meet you, Jason. If you don't mind, my friends and I were going to get moving, lots to do today. You stay safe, okay?"

Taking the hint, Jason stepped back and raised the water bottle in salute. "Yeah, thanks Katelyn, I appreciate it." He turned and headed back up the path.

Katelyn followed him with her eyes until he turned out of sight. "It's all right, Jessica," she comforted without turning toward her. "He's harmless."

Jessica nodded.

"What is the problem?" Dee asked.

"My dad. Homeless people are drawn to him because he stands out so much." Jessica held her hand up above her head showing his height relative to hers. He was significantly taller than she, as tall as Poke. "My whole life, whenever we go out, someone is hitting him up for money or food. It makes me nervous."

"Has anything happened? The man acted non-threatening, despite his appearance." Dee's fist unclenched.

"No, nothing ever has. But you didn't walk away this time," Katelyn answered for her. She smiled and quickly squeezed Jessica's hand.

"Why are there people without homes?" Dee started back in its line of questioning.

"Haven't you already read about it? Haven't you already read, like, the entire internet? What is KT looking for anyway?" Jessica asked.

"I would like to hear it from your perspective. KT has its own qualifications, none of which I am privy too. I am its adjutant, not its superior. We further know that your internet cannot possibly contain everything important in Terran culture. You have always been secretive of embarrassing information."

"It's a complicated issue," Jessica started to explain. "Some people lose their jobs and can't afford to live anywhere. Others are running from a bad life, or are hooked on drugs or alcohol. A lot have mental disorders that aren't treated well. Sometimes the cards are stacked against them. There are about as many reasons as you can think of. And some folks… some folks wanna check out of the whole system because it's crazy." Jessica nodded in Jason's direction.

"Are there no places where he could get food and shelter without having to beg for it?"

"Yeah, there are, but it's a pretzel, and we have plenty," Katelyn said, holding up the other golden-brown loop.

Chapter 29: The Prize

The four walked out onto the Bow Bridge, dodging other tourists. Dee scanned the surroundings, as if its neck were a swivel. Several times it walked up to groups of children a bit too closely for their parents' comfort.

"What is this game you are playing?" it asked a pair of small girls, who immediately put on the New York cold stare.

"Mami says not to talk to strangers," one commented, picking up her Pokémon cards and heading to the other side of the bridge. Her friend trailed behind her, never taking her eyes off the android.

He followed them without hesitation, asking the same question until Katelyn interceded.

"Dee, you have to be a bit subtler than that, you're freaking people out," she explained, her voice low.

Jessica stepped up between the groups, and addressed the girls with a smile. "It's okay, he's… a little slow. He didn't mean to scare you."

The first girl peeked around Jessica and studied Dee, who stared back, imploringly.

"He's strange," the second girl scoffed.

"Your mom is right; don't talk to strangers, especially men." It broke her heart to have to tell them something nearly every woman learns throughout the course of her young life. She also realized the hypocrisy of the statement since she was a stranger to them as well. She exercised the unwritten rule of safety among women. Still, she kept her distance.

"I do not understand," Dee commented to Katelyn, after she refused to allow him a step further. "I am merely gathering information on a game in which I do not know the rules. How else am I to learn it? The children of The People do not recoil when another approaches them."

"Dee… how do I…?" Jessica fumbled to find an explanation other than blurting out: "Because there are sexual predators who would love to get their hands on children," without making the Terrans into monsters yet again. She didn't want to lie. "Children don't normally deal with adults in an informal way. If you haven't been introduced, you don't talk to them."

Is it just New Yorkers that are like this? Are we really all this way?

"But you are speaking to them, and you have not been introduced," it stated flatly.

Jessica took a breath as she and Katelyn began to shuffle Dee off the bridge as the girls' older brother stepped up and collected them. She scanned the shoreline and saw their mother looking on from a bench, her face calm, but her eyes were wide with worry. Jessica raised her hand and waved to her, nodding as she did so. The mother relaxed.

"This is a strange world. You speak to someone who potentially could be dangerous, then you do not speak to children who are not." Dee turned around facing over The Lake, looking in the direction of the homeless man Jason, who was in the process of hitting up a group of tourists for money.

"Everyone is completely safe on all of your worlds? No one is ever in danger?" Jessica asked, incredulous.

"We have evolved beyond the need for violence. There is no scarcity among us. No one need suffer for anything," the android answered her, the pride in its voice apparent as it spoke. From behind it, Katelyn raised her eyebrows and rattled her head side to side mockingly. From all the years that she'd know her, Jessica was sure Katelyn would have used a phrase akin to, "Well, aren't we pleased with ourselves?" She suppressed a laugh at the sight.

"Explain to me, why is there still scarcity on your world? When I visited last we expected it since the society was primitive and backward. Did something happen to set this world back? Something you are afraid to put on display in your internet?"

Dee and Jessica stepped off the bridge and continued down the path. The sun felt warm despite the chilly air. From her own world, Jessica knew that it could snow almost any day at this point in the year, but it rarely happened before Christmas anymore. She had yet to revisit a "normal" holiday season, post-pandemic. She'd forgotten what it was like. Large groups still frightened her to some extent, and she never left her apartment without her mask. Secretly, she worried a Terran variant existed that ignored its vaccine, or a more virulent variant existed here, and she could bring it back home. She didn't talk about it, fearing the knowledge would root itself in her psyche and hound every quiet moment.

Jessica explained, "Things happen, I don't know all of Terran history. It's probably capitalism or something. We all fight for resources and money. A lot of people have a lot, and a lot don't have anything. Add a random event and things don't always go the way you want."

"Jason refused your system, yet he does not mind asking for things that he needs. He still accumulates wealth, in a small way. Does he not?"

Jessica stopped on the path and turned to look at the opposite shore, watching Jason asking for money.

"I don't know, but they shouldn't have to beg for food. It's no way for anyone to live." Jessica scanned the bridge, looking for something to take her mind off such a heavy subject. She saw Poke and Katelyn leaning over the side. Katelyn was pointing to the fish that knew to swim up where they could also beg for food. Invariably someone would throw them something. They grew accustomed to it, and in some ways, it was easier for the fish to simply beg than hunt for bugs, or pluck at the murky bottom of The Lake.

"This isn't helping," Jessica muttered to herself. She smiled at another group of children running along the shore, playing a game with sticks and flicking pebbles into the lake. Dee looked on inquisitively and she waved the android off.

"What happened before the Singularity? What was the Hegemony like before you all came online?"

Dee looked away from the children, keen to respond to the direct question. "There are not many records that exist from that time. Our society was barbaric and primitive. We do know that the Takki still consumed animal flesh."

Ahh, that's where the order came from, Jessica thought, looking at Poke and Katelyn still on the bridge. He was consuming yet another hot dog.

"There were several ethnic groups that fought amongst themselves. Obviously, the lack of a unified government prevented them from achieving the peace the Hegemony would eventually bring. Wars were not common; however, there was little regard for differing cultures and opinions."

Jessica saw an opening and took it. "You're comparing us to where you were before you became 'enlightened,' aren't you? Whether you think, or KT thinks, that we are somehow redeemable. So, whose culture is The Hegemony really? Who won?"

"Won? I do not understand you. The People 'won' by being unified and no longer fighting." Dee cocked its head like a dog hearing a strange sound.

"The word Hegemony, it means dominance by one group, right? So, someone won. Who was it?"

"You are implying some sort of ethnic cleansing or genocide are you not?" Dee questioned, without much in the way of emotion in its voice.

"Walks like a duck," Jessica commented, with a nod.

"Duck? All the ducks I see in the lake are currently swimming. Can you see waterfowl that I do not?"

"Dee, give me a break. You're standing there questioning my culture when yours has obviously done something reprehensible in the past. Spare me the sanctimony." Her voice quavered as she finished her statement.

"I did not mean to upset you. I was merely answering your question and I presented the facts as I know them. Our society became unified during the Singularity. There was no desire for control or dominance, only the acceptance of the illogic of division and waste. The only prize was peace and reason."

Jessica looked around the lake. A beautiful October afternoon brought everyone out to enjoy the weather. Central Park was, by design, the backyard for the people of Manhattan. Every culture that she knew of were represented here. Varied, mixed, embracing. Infinite diversity, infinite combination. Were they all destined to become one gigantic culture? A stew with dozens of textures and flavors, or one grey ooze with no variety?

"So, in the end, there can be only one, huh?"

Dee regarded her coolly, its face still warm and inviting, but its eyes were cold, without emotion. Moments like this reminded her this was a mechanism and not a biological organism. A chilled breeze blew off the lake, and Jessica pulled her hoodie up tighter.

"The Hegemony is one. Inseparable," responded the android.

Chapter 30: All Hallows' Eve

"That's not a convincing costume, Gaian. You do not look like the agreed upon image of a ghost on this world," Dee spoke to Jessica, as it analyzed her clothing. Its face was painted green, and two "bolts" were drawn on the neck in black paint.

Jessica was dressed in a white sheet, with two eyeholes cut out. She considered going with the "Charlie Brown" costume with multiple black holes, but was unsure if this planet had the same version of the cartoon she had grown up with.

"Dee, Halloween is not about looking exactly like what they look like, but what your interpretation is. I don't think Shelley had you in mind when she envisioned the monster, but you do kinda look like Karlof." Jessica explained, trying to move silently across the carpet without ruffling the bottom of the white sheet, "Besides, I'm dead, remember, and people might recognize me since we're staying in the neighborhood. What better costume?"

"Unless she comes for you," Katelyn commented nonchalantly.

"Hey, I've been sleeping in her bed for three days. If she had an issue with me, I think she would have let me know by now. I'm not dressed up like her anyway."

Poke, without a costume or glasses, walked out of the kitchen with a large bowl of pasta and a salad fork. He balanced the bowl gingerly as he made his way over to the table.

"Have some food there, big guy!" Katelyn commented as he passed her.

"I need to have energy!" Peek chimed in from the pocket in Poke's jeans relaying his speech. "This will be a long night of walking around, apparently."

"What are we to do with all of this candy?" Dee inquired, staring down at the bowl, "We are not expected to eat it?"

"No, silly!" Katelyn scooped up the bowl of assorted "fun-sized" candies. "These are for the kids. We're too old to eat this." She promptly pulled out a package of malt balls, and in one motion opened them up and ate the triplet of candies. Poke laughed, in his own voice. Katelyn winked.

A knock came from the door, and Katelyn sprung to it. Cracking the door slowly she croaked in a raspy voice, "Yesssss….?"

In the hallway two children, one dressed as a cowboy and another as a mummy, timidly croaked, "T-trick or Treat!" and held out their pillowcase bags, already containing a fairly respectable haul.

Katelyn flung wide the door. "And why should I give you my candy? What will you do if I don't?"

The children stood there, unsure of what to do.

Katelyn knelt down, and addressed them quietly, "Trick or Treat is a threat, kids. When the person doesn't give you a treat, you're supposed to threaten them with a trick."

Jessica rolled her eyes and threw out her hands. "Every year."

Without turning back, Katelyn answered, "If they don't understand the rules, how are they supposed to pass the tradition on?"

The children stood there, the cowboy staring blankly, and the mummy glancing back and forth.

"What do you say?" Katelyn implored.

"Trick or Treat?" they implored again in unison.

Frustrated, Katelyn reached into the bowl and pulled two handfuls of candy out, giving them each half in turn.

"Here, remember this for next year, right?" She dismissed the children, who obliged by quickly turning down the hall and knocking on another door.

"Trick or Treat!" they announced loudly at another door as Katelyn closed the one to the apartment.

"Kids these days, I can't."

Poke dropped the salad fork into the bowl, and asked via Peek, "When do we leave?"

"When Dad gets here. He usually watches the door when we go out."

"I don't understand, aren't we too old?"

"We don't go Trick or Treating, but we like to go out when the kids are out. It's fun," Jessica answered.

"I haven't gone door-to-door in a long time," Katelyn said as she pulled a yellow coat out of the closet.

Jessica threw the ghost costume up over her head so she could see more clearly. "This is cool. You will get to be aliens out in the open. Don't try to do anything weird, okay? And follow my lead if you get confused."

Peek answered for Poke, "Yes, Jessica." Peek then spoke for itself, using the higher voice of the assistant on the smartphone, "Yay! Kids! Candy!"

Jessica curtsied, ignoring the fact Peek had no idea of what candy meant to a child. "I think you'll like what you see. This is all about the kids."

Dee turned its gold-irised eyes to her, "The Romans had several rituals to mark the passage of the dead. None of these involved children. I understand the genesis of this ritual, but I do not understand why children, who have so much to live for, would be obsessed with the dead."

Katelyn answered, "Dude, I've said this a dozen times before, it's not about death. It's about dressing up, being 'fun-scared,' and getting candy. You think about this too much."

"I am merely attempting to ascertain whether your culture understands the implication of death and its significance in the cycle of all things."

"Poke? Did you play games like this as a child?" Jessica inquired.

Carrying the bowl to the sink, Poke answered. "We didn't celebrate death. When you die, you either just die, or we upload you to the network where you can live forever. Like Peek. I don't know anyone who is 'gone.' They're all still here."

Peek flashed from his temple, and then chimed in as well, "I died. Old. Long ago. Bigger now!"

"You mean you're bigger since you're walking around in a phone?" Jessica responded, with a hint of irony.

"Cozy," Peek replied, its LED flickering in its "laugh" pattern.

The was a knock at the door and Jessica answered, Ellwood strode in dressed as a -much older - version of Marty McFly, replete with double-sunburst ties, brown shirt, and coat. Katelyn stepped out of the bedroom dressed as the 2015 version of Doc Brown, yellow overcoat and double plastic ties.

"Run for it, Marty!" she yelled.

Jessica laughed at the interplay between the two, as if Katelyn were his second daughter. *In a way, she is.* "Old Marty doesn't have a beard," she said, examining his costume.

"Yes, he does," he answered without missing a beat.

"No, he doesn't, it would make it hard to tell he was the same Marty unless…"

"I guess that's another difference huh?" Katelyn asked, fixing "Marty's" ties.

Jessica frowned, not wanting to feel the pain of feeling different yet again. She folded her ghost costume back over her face and put her keys in her pocket.

"Okay guys, let's do this!" She said, attempting to feel chipper. The four of them headed out the apartment door, letting Ellwood take the reins in the apartment for a bit. In the elevator, children from the other floors gawked at the two aliens with awe, commenting they had never seen costumes so good before. They exited with an entourage of small admirers.

"Be careful, children," Dee cautioned as they went their separate ways when leaving the building.

They headed past the light-rail station and toward Kennedy Boulevard, the same path they took every year. Eventually they would head up the four-lane street to her mother's house. The girls decided they would not go all the way this year so as not to upset her. She still didn't know, and introducing Jessica from another dimension -on Halloween of all nights- might be too much to for her to bear.

A perfect October night greeted them, the crisp air with a slight bite, partly cloudy, and a sliver of moon. The streets were filled with children going door to door and begging for treats, a movie-set level of perfection.

Dee scanned the interaction while Peek and Poke recorded everything.

Children ran and laughed, and Jessica completely forgot the fact she was on an alien world, in an alien dimension, and an alien herself.

"Is this the same on your world?" Dee asked.

"Yep, but not as cheery as this. It's kinda odd. Or maybe I've gotten too cynical," Jessica responded, then shrugged.

Katelyn smiled and skipped, running up behind a group of children calling, "I'm gonna get ya!" They tore up the sidewalk, squealing.

"And you ignore all that is going on in the world around you? Even if it is dangerous?"

"A few years back there was this story about this guy putting razor blades into the treats. I remember metal detectors and stuff. All kinds of depressing," Jessica explained. "Turned out to be a hoax, but the next year all the candy companies made small candies they could sell to nervous parents. A few years later you didn't see traditional treats anymore, like candied apples or popcorn balls. All the candy became 'fun-sized.' Ironically, copycats put pins in those. Idiots." Jessica felt a twinge of anxiety as she realized that last statement didn't paint humans in a good light.

"Commercialism. Bah!" groaned Katelyn, as she threw candies to a few children who were a bit too old to be out.

"Still, it didn't change anything. Even with COVID we still had people out on their porches giving candy away. No one touched each other, but they still talked and laughed. We were still a community, maybe stronger than before." She stepped lightly, reveling in the memory.

Poke laughed without a translation as other children tumbled up a front porch crying, "They have full-sized bars!"

Dee nodded silently, as Peek flashed its laugh.

Coming to the corner of Claremont and Kennedy Boulevard, several groups of children queued, waiting to cross. The older children waited patiently, with the younger ones anxious to cross. A black van sat idling, too close to the corner for comfort; it narrowed the street, forcing everyone to cross between it and the parked cars.

"¡No, cuidado mijo!" a woman yelled to her son, dressed as the Red Power Ranger. He kept trying to pull away from her arm as she simultaneously corralled his siblings.

"¡MIJO!" she yelled.

Jessica turned around to see the child dash into the street, as a delivery truck, going much too fast for the small street, turned the corner.

In a flash, Dee ran into the street, grabbed the child, and turned its back toward the oncoming truck. The sick sound of screeching tires and crunching metal filled the air.

"DEE!" Jessica and Katelyn yelled. Poke took a step back and reached out for them.

"DON'T!" He called out in Standard, scaring the onlookers further.

Wreckage was strewn about the street and smoke from the burning tires mixed with escaping water vapor from the truck's engine. The children on either corner screamed, and punctuated above them, the panicked cries of the mother.

When the smoke did clear, Dee stood in the middle of the street with the child held securely in its arms. The child wailed hysterically but was completely unhurt. Dee's clothes and were torn from its back, revealing servos and wires which strained and bulged out of the imitation flesh. Green paint smeared down its face, revealing more damage to its synthetic skin. The truck wrapped around the pair in a "U," it's radiator spilling water onto the pavement.

"¡MIJO!" the woman screamed again, rushing into the street to claim her charge.

Jessica and Katelyn moved to join her, but Poke forcefully pulled them back. Peek spoke from the smartphone as loudly as the speaker would allow, "NO! Must hide!"

The woman pulled her child from the android's arms. She didn't notice its exposed body, or see the sparks erupting from its back, its eyes a solid electric blue.

"Gracias! Thank you for saving him!" She wept and ran back onto the sidewalk.

"My pleasure, madam," Dee answered and then climbed the wreckage to assist the driver.

"You have been involved in an accident and you require assistance," it addressed the terrified driver, who pushed himself back from the windshield, blood pouring from a gash on his forehead. Dee immediately put its hand onto the driver's head to stop the bleeding. Its arm twitched as the sound of grating servos filled the air.

Jessica could physically feel the dozens of people with their cellphones trained on the scene recording the incident from every angle. She knew the footage would be online for the whole world to see in a matter of moments. EMS sirens wailed in the distance, drawing ever closer.

"We have to get out of here." She reached back to grab Poke's restraining arm. "They will see us."

The area around the truck filled with adults and teens recording every second of the interaction. Dee yelled from the cab, its voice commanding and blue irises sweeping across the crowd like a searchlight.

"This area is dangerous, please leave or you may be injured."

"What do we do? We can't leave him! Do your people just abandon your friends?" Katelyn spat, still fighting Poke's restraint.

Peek answered her directly, "Protocol. It ignores us. Not abandon. We find. We get back."

The trio turned on their heels and ran back down the street.

Chapter 31: The Plan

The five assembled sat in the living room contemplating the situation. Only two of the five actually belonged there, the others were alien in both location and species. All of them were now focused on saving a completely artificial life form that risked its life, as well as detection, to save an errant human child.

"So, what do we do here? Is this like *The X-files?* Are we going to have to to go to New Mexico or something to get him? When do you think the feds are going to show up and dissect him?" Katelyn mused aloud.

"Friend Katelyn," Poke spoke from the smartphone, which was now plugged to recharge as quickly as possible, "Dee does not use a gender. It simply is. You would not like to be called 'him' when you aren't." He turned to Katelyn, another bowl of pasta in his large hands. Katelyn nodded in acquiescence.

"So how do we find *it*?" she reiterated.

Jessica came out of the kitchen with two mugs of hot coffee and handed one to her best friend. "Peek mentioned a protocol?" she asked Poke, after taking a large swig from the cup. He answered in Standard, and Peek did not translate.

"We established when we first came to this world, if any of us were to be captured, we would not reveal our identity. Of course, we'd say we were gods which would get us… off the hook? There is no way Dee would give us away. That's why I pulled us out as fast as possible so we could maintain the illusion. We're not allowed to retrieve our friend and are supposed to find the best way to keep hidden and free ourselves. If that can't happen… we're to remove all evidence, including ourselves." Poke cast his glance to the floor, his grey skin and completely green eyes more apparent than ever. Jessica knew what that meant.

"But you're not gods now," Jessica said as she plopped down on the couch, taking another swig of coffee.

"No, we aren't…" Poke leaned back as if he were listening to someone speaking over his shoulder. He raised his index finger to let the women know he was talking to Peek in private. The LEDs in his temple flashed furiously.

"How does that keep us safe? Huh," he responded to Peek aloud, then grew quiet as the conversation got more in-depth.

Ellwood, still dressed as Old Marty, absentmindedly stroked the two ties hung around his neck. He looked listlessly out of the window, lost in his own thoughts. Katelyn twitched from the lack of activity. Jessica looked from one to the other.

"We have to find Dee, we have to get it out. The more time we waste, the harder it will be. Poke? Have you located it yet?" she asked.

Poke raised his finger again, LEDs still flashing wildly.

She turned her head in frustration. They sat there helplessly, unable to make a move with their limited information.

Ellwood pulled out of his reverie. "It was probably taken to the police station, or the hospital. We need to get it out of there."

"How do we do that?" Jessica mimicked a Jersey City police officer. "'Yeah so eh… we gots dis robut alien and uhhhh, I dunno what to freakin' do wit 'em. You wan't 'em?' I really don't see how this is going to work."

"Can we pay them off? How much you got saved up?" Katelyn quickly asked Ellwood.

"Just the money we had saved up to finish the rest of grad school for her." Ellwood pointed to Terran Jessica's room, and not to the alien one sitting next to her.

"Are we talking about bribery here? Actually bribing police to get an android out of lockup? Does that make any sense?" Jessica asked the pair, stressing each word.

"What choice do we have?" Katelyn shot back.

The three started talking over each other, getting progressively louder by the moment, going nowhere. Poke banged on the side of the pasta bowl with a pair of chopsticks, getting their attention.

"Friends, Peek has found Dee. It is transmitting on an encoded frequency, very faint, but we see it."

They all sat quietly for a moment, wrapped up in the futility of the situation. Jessica broke the silence. "Peek, where is it now?"

"A… warehouse. In place called 'Port Newark,'" Poke said from the phone.

"Shit," Jessica blurted out reflexively. "That's not the cops."

Katelyn's brow furrowed.

"Da… Ellwood, why would our friend be taken to a warehouse in Port Newark? Unless…"

"Unless they don't want to be found."

"Peek?" Jessica inquired.

"Looking. Not police. Advanced. Encryptions, solar power, wind turbines. Hidden," the AI responded from the smartphone. It stopped speaking and flashed with Poke. He closed his eyes at the torrent of data, and after a moment he came around.

"Whoever they are, they know what they are doing… well, for Terran technology. I mean no disrespect," Poke explained.

Katelyn snapped her head up. "That black van! The one that was at the corner, I saw it at Central Park! I knew it!"

Ellwood nodded. "Great, some black-ops hacker group. They probably think Dee is government and wants to ransom him… it."

"So, do we call the police?" Katelyn chimed in.

"No, it would be worse. They could be feds too, which… who knows what they would do," Ellwood said.

"You said you posed as gods to protect your identity. Right?" Jessica asked.

Poke nodded.

"Then we're going to have to hope they are *X-Files fans*." Jessica's hands started to shake visibly, but a crooked smile crossed her face.

Katelyn stood up and toasted her bestie. "I like where this is going!"

"Button, do you think…"

"Don't worry, Ellwood. I have a plan."

Chapter 32: The Truth Is Way Out There

Jessica walked up to the warehouse. Its nondescript building stood in rows of other similar buildings. The big distinction was a high chain-link fence and security bollards. A single sign on the front read: "Transglobal Shipping." Everything about the building said, "go away."

A front for a legitimate business of course.

She whispered into her shoulder, "You guys getting this?"

"We are, Friend Jessica. Ready when you are," Poke's voice whispered in her ear.

A gust of wind blew past her face, like the flapping of wings.

Jessica nodded and stepped through the front doors of the building and into the vestibule, taking notice of all the security cameras focused on her. As she approached the front desk, she scanned the layout. Two black-uniformed security guards sat behind plexiglass shielding, which she presumed was bullet-proof. They were armed. Behind them she could see the rows of shipping crates, and maps of various major cities around the world. A white sign with the company slogan draped across the opening of a single door:

"Transglobal Shipping: We get it there."

She desperately fought the urge to turn and run out of the door. Dressed in Terran Jessica's black restaurant uniform, she exuded ulterior motive. Taking a deep breath, she stepped forward.

"Hi, I'm here looking for a package of mine. It was brought in recently. A statue of my father. It's very lifelike, tall dude, blond hair. Kinda cute."

The left guard looked up from his desk and slid his tablet to the side.

"Hello," he said cautiously. "I'm sorry, this is only for shipping out, we don't receive here. What was the name on the package, perhaps I can find where it was sent?" He smiled broadly, almost genuinely. Jessica's anxiety hyper-focused on the situation at hand, and she saw the slightest doubt in his eyes. She shook internally at the question; her blood ran cold. They had never thought of a name for Dee other than Dee.

"Dee … adju… lia… Liaison."

"Dee Liaison?" the security guard asked, standing up from his chair, holding the tablet.

"Yes, that's his name, all right. From the Murry Hill Liaisons. It's French."

The other guard focused on Jessica, and she could feel his eyes boring into the side of her head. The first guard looked at his tablet perfunctorily, tapped a few buttons, and then dropped it back on his desk.

"There is no shipment under that name, sweetheart. You're not at the right building."

"Um, this is the Port Newark office. It should've arrived here an hour or so ago."

The other officer stood up from his desk. The one she had been speaking to reached down for the buzzer to open the plexiglass door between them.

"Stay where you are miss," he said as he walked around the desk and stepped through the doorway. He placed his hand on the taser strapped just below his pistol. The other guard locked the front door with the press of another buzzer.

Jessica smiled at the first guard, "Do you think that's really necessary? All I want is my package and then I can go."

"I'm afraid that isn't possible. Turn around and put your hands behind your head."

"Sigh," Jessica said aloud. "It would've been much easier if you'd just done what I asked."

"I doubt it," the officer said as he reached for her right arm.

The building plunged into darkness. Safety lights flashed on. Alarms blared.

The guard grabbed at Jessica's wrist. He looked down in shock as he came up with nothing but air. Jessica was nowhere to be seen. "What the hell?"

The second guard ran from behind the desk, for a moment they stood dumbfounded as the strobe lights from the alarm system pierced the darkness.

BOOM! came from the front door; both guards drew their guns and pointed.

A second of silence. Then another *BOOM.*

The door to the back office opened, and two men in black fatigues, fully armored and armed with shotguns, ran up behind them.

"What? Where'd the girl go? What is it?" One of the new officers scanned the security monitors across from the desks, all of which displayed Peek's smiling yellow emoji.

"What the…?"

BOOM!

They turned to the front door and opened fire.

Jessica strode into the back room with security running past her. They were all heavily armored, some brandished assault rifles.

"Please don't let anyone get hurt. In and out," she whispered to herself.

A guard stopped and turned to face her, he squinted and searched for the source of the voice. Jessica froze and held her breath.

He tilted his head in one direction, then the other. "Hello?" he said, barely audible over the gunfire from the front of the station, a slight whistle coming from his missing teeth. He raised his gun, not sure of what he was aiming at.

Jessica held herself motionless and stared right into the guard's eyes. She recognized him, Jason, the homeless man from Central Park. Her confusion switched to rage at having been deceived, especially after helping him. She lifted a trembling, unseen fist, and steeled herself to contact his face.

"Jay! Come on!" yelled another voice from the front of the station.

"Right!" he called out and lowered the gun, running to the front.

As she walked to the back of the building, Jessica noticed security monitors at regular intervals along the walls. In one monitor she saw a hallway which resembled hers, and peering intently, she could not see herself on the screen. Satisfied her invisibility was working, she looked at another monitor to check on her companions. In the front of the building, Poke raised his arms over his head. "I'm going to eat you!" he roared in his native language, which came out as a series of grunts and barks.

Bullet rounds flew toward him, then stopped suddenly, dropping to the floor harmlessly. He paced back and forth uttering random taunts; "I will eat your pasta! You smell like lavender! You don't understand temporal mechanics." Then, the coup de gras of insults which he learned from Katelyn, "Yankees suck!" He did his best to suppress his laughter.

The security guards arrayed themselves around the front door, laying Poke in the middle of a crossfire. Every single round flew toward him at devastating speed, only to stop inches from his body. The dullest "thud" could be heard before the rounds clinked on the ground at his feet.

The lights flashed and alarms went on and off at random times, doors opened and closed. The sounds of Peek laughing peeled over the loudspeakers.

The room slowly filled with smoke from the expended rounds. Hot bullet casings drummed on the floor.

Jessica hurried to the back of the building. Nestled among myriad shipping crates, computer equipment abounded. Displays showed streams of data, and surveillance screens of dozens of locations flicked between monitors. All the major news networks and hundreds of websites and social media feeds dominated every inch of screen real estate. Information flowed like water.

"This is not good. Who are these guys?" she said out loud.

About to turn a corner, Jessica stopped as another video feed caught her eye. She stepped up to it, squinting to focus in the sensory overload. "Son of a..." she gasped.

The screen showed, very clearly, the light-rail station the three of them had hacked into days before. It rolled back and forth, showing Jessica moving between them and blocking the camera. Poke and Dee were clearly visible before the screen went dark.

"They saw us, they've been tracking us the whole time."

She glanced around, concerned that she was tipping her hand by recognizing herself, fully forgetting that she was still invisible. In the back of the room, she saw several faces hiding behind computer screens. They looked about her age, wearing various forms of "hacker chic," some behind monitors or tablets, others recording on their smartphones. One in particular, a man about thirty - bald save for an eagle tattoo on the right side of his head - kept scanning the room, as if he saw something the others didn't. Jessica moved on feeling better to leave instead of standing there and potentially giving herself away. She walked forward down the hallway that stretched behind the bank of screens. Doors unlocked and swung open without her having to touch them thanks to Peek's complete control of their security system. Stepping gently, she made no sound.

Another guard desk appeared, and another security guard stood with a shotgun, scanning the area. An open room just to the side of him flashed lights; out of it she could hear Peek humming, "Itsy Bitsy Spider," over the loudspeakers. She could tell it was doing its best to create confusion. A nursery rhyme was a nice touch. The closer she got to the guard, the more nervous she became. She gasped when a large dog rounded the corner.

"Stop! Don't move!" the guard commanded, pointing the shotgun directly at her head. Instinctively she ducked and backed off. The dog stepped forward, waiting for the command to attack.

Taking another breath, she raised her hands and concentrated on projecting the antigravity field ahead of her. As it moved out, she could feel herself getting heavier as the wings shunted energy to her hands. She prayed she wouldn't suddenly become visible.

Pull to my hand.

In an instant the shotgun tore from the guard's hand and flew into her own, still suspended in the field. Having never held a gun before, she quickly slid it across the floor out of reach. As she turned her attention back, she heard him give the command to attack.

The German Shepherd leapt from the floor with lightning speed. On instinct, she threw her hands in front of her face and turned her head. The dog dropped to the floor with a yelp of surprise. It bit into the air in several locations that would have found their mark if it were not for the antigravity field around her.

"Heel!" the guard yelled, trying to get control of the situation again.

The dog backed off, twisting its head back and forth, fixing its eyes on her face.

It can see me.

"Who are you? Show yourself!" the guard commanded, pulling his sidearm.

Concentrating again Jessica envisioned the field flattening out in front of her, and she pushed with her hands, forcing both the guard and the dog into the open room. With a yelp from the dog, Jessica slammed the door behind them and locked it. From all the effort, the antigravity field shut off and she fell to the floor, completely visible.

With her wing's power shut off momentarily, she got up and physically lifted the desk, laying it down across the hallway, wedging the door closed.

"That's not going to hold them long," she muttered.

Concentrating, Jessica enveloped the field around her again. Invisible, she ran down the hallway as fast as she could.

"Left, right, left again," she said, reminding herself of the directions Peek had given her after it had hacked into the satellite dish on the roof.

"Friend Jessica, you must hurry!" Jessica heard Poke yell into her headset. She glanced at a security monitor, its flickering screen showing the chaos at the front of the building.

Poke danced through a hail of bullets that slowly began to accumulate at his feet like lead snow. "They aren't giving up. I think they're getting desperate… WHAT? You're kidding me!" Poke yelled as Jessica spun away from the monitor and sprinted down the hall.

Peek repeated to both of them with excitement rising in its synthetic voice, "Government. Big truck. Many guns. Coming!"

"Jessica, HURRY!" Poke screamed into his microphone.

Jessica turned one last corner and saw a solid black door with no markings and a security card reader. Just the one she wanted. Without hesitating, she turned off the invisibility, picked up speed, and plowed at the door as hard as she could.

With a splinter of metal and wood, the door exploded as she smashed through it. Laptops and other computer equipment scattered around the room, cameras focused from every angle. Steel bars separated the space she was in from the form of Dee, who sat forlornly on a bed.

"Dee! It's me, let's go!"

Dee turned toward Jessica and addressed her, speaking in Standard.

"What are you doing here, Jessica? Did Peek not inform you of the protocol?" The question was more admonishment than inquiry.

"Yeah, it did, we decided to get you anyway."

"If anyone was injured… you should not have come… if you are captured…" Dee desperately tried to explain and command at the same time.

"Shut up!"

Pulling the antigravity field toward her, Jessica concentrated on the recording devices scattered around the room. With a flick of her fingers, the cameras flew off the walls and tripods smashed to the floor. Satisfied they were no longer being recorded, she pulled Dee's gold cube out of her pocket and tossed it.

With android dexterity, Dee caught the cube and unfolded it, the wingspan nearly filling the entire room.

"Keep 'em folded, it's really tight in the hallways."

Dee nodded.

"Okay, let's take care of these guys." She wagged her finger at the bars.

With combined pulls, the pair tore the steel door open, allowing Dee to step through.

"Thank you for rescuing me, Jessica."

Jessica started and gazed over Dee's face. It looked the most human she had ever seen it, despite streaked green paint, exposed actuators, and torn synthetic flesh. Genuine gratitude was displayed in a wide smile.

She smiled back. "No problem. Come on, follow my lead."

Dee's irises flashed blue then the two ran down the hallway back the way she'd come.

"This distraction they are providing; it is very illogical and potentially dangerous. There must have been an easier way?" Dee asked as they scrambled around the corner.

"We didn't have the time. I don't know tactics well. It's my first prison break, go easy on me," she said, panting between sentences.

When they turned the corner, they ran right into the guards coming in the other direction.

"Stop!" Jason commanded, an assault rifle in his hand. He was flanked by two other guards, both armed with shotguns.

Jessica looked down at her body. She was fully visible. In her excitement, she forgot to re-engage the light bending property of the antigravity field. The field was still on though, she could feel it. She cleared her throat. She could have pulled the weapons away and tossed Jason and his people around like ragdolls. Or turned their bullets back on themselves, or a myriad of forceful actions. She decided to use as little power as necessary and get them to willingly comply.

"Jason do not be afraid. We come in peace and no harm will come to you. You know us to be compassionate." Jessica puffed her chest up as big as she could, Dee followed suit, unsure of exactly how to be intimidating.

"Right," he replied while the sounds of gunfire in the front of the building suddenly stopped.

"JESSICA! NOW!" she heard Poke scream and Peek squealed in her ear, "Big truck! Big gun!"

Jessica's gaze darted to the front of the warehouse. Behind Poke and the mounds of spent rounds, the door to the station shone bright white. Behind the glare, she could see an armored assault vehicle. A .50-caliber gun slowly emerged; the SWAT acronym emblazoned on the side. This had to end now, before someone got hurt.

"Jason, you don't have to do this. We know that you resent authority, we know that you don't like the system. Those are Feds outside. What can you accomplish by keeping us here? You know they will take all of us and you won't get whatever it is you desire. Lay down your weapons and allow us to pass."

"I can't let you do that," he responded, and pulled back the bolt on his rifle.

"What do you want from us?" she asked.

"I want to know who you are, where you come from. All that technology you have. You aren't from here. You're proof that the government is lying to us."

Jessica tried to think as fast as she could, desperate to find a way out of the situation without her having to hurt anyone. She looked to the back of the room where the same techs were still standing, recording everything that was transpiring. She did her best to seem believable.

"Jason, we are not from your world, and your government does not know of us. We work alone. You have heard of us in your past. Ancient stories of gods and monsters. We are your myths. The stories you tell your children. We exist in shadow, never in one place for long, but always watching. We slip in and out of your reality as easily as you slip into a dream. We are unbound."

A chill ran down Jessica's spine as she almost believed what she was saying, and in a way, it was true.

"I said stop. Now."

"We will not harm you. You *will* let us pass," Jessica reiterated, trying to sound as regal as possible.

With that, she unfolded her wings in a flash and lifted herself off the floor. A full meter into the air, they caught the light from the truck, and the room bathed in green and white. Dee followed suit, adding gold to the brilliance.

Jason's rifle hit the ground with a clatter and he stood transfixed.

"Allow us to pass."

Without speaking, Jason and the other guards stepped back and let the pair float by. Jessica and Dee held their heads high, attempting to appear unconcerned with the thoughts of mortal men.

When Poke saw them floating into the main area, he also unfolded his wings and lifted from the floor.

When the trio was reunited, the warehouse, the assault vehicle, and the streetlights for the entire neighborhood went out. Everything was plunged into darkness.

The doors opened and closed silently.

The world sprang back into light.

They were gone.

Chapter 33: All Saints' Day

"Ellwood, are you receiving?" Jessica asked.

"Loud and clear Button, how did it go?"

Jessica smiled as the trio circled the warehouse, gaining altitude as they did. The SWAT team flooded into the building as several other vans arrived on the scene. Helicopter blades thundered in the distance. "That is the beginning of a long day for our friends, but mission accomplished," She responded.

Jessica looked over at Dee and Poke, the shimmer of the antigravity blending them in with the view. She gave the two the thumbs-up, but then realized they didn't know of the modern use of the gesture. Nor could they see her anyway.

"Great!" Ellwood exclaimed.

"We'll meet you at the rendezvous in half an hour," Jessica responded to him. She glanced over at Dee's lights and saw blue sparks spilling into the air.

"Can you bring extra clothes? Something bulky. Dee is pretty beat up. We will get there as fast as we can," Jessica said as the trio banked east toward the Hudson.

"Can do! See you soon. Be safe."

Jessica flinched at his use of the COVID benediction. There should be two Jessicas here, yet there was only one. Everyone had a double but her. She wasn't even from this dimension, cut off and yet still part of three universes.

I am unbound.

"Poke? Let's head over."

He responded into her earbud, "Okay!"

They flew until they hovered over the same spot they had arrived in at Liberty State Park, landing silently behind a copse of pine trees, the one her father had picnicked with her on countless occasions.

Poke took off his wings and pocketed the square, and helped Dee take off the golden pair.

"How do you feel?" he asked, examining Dee's torn back. There was absolutely no hiding it; even bulky clothes would not be able to conceal the damage. Dee's right scapula held on by a single actuator, which protested loudly each time its shoulders moved. It hung out like a shark's fin. The android's neck sparked below the right ear, causing the eye to uncontrollably twitch when it flashed. The ear hung on by the aesthetic artificial flesh holding it there, its microphone clearly visible. The alloy jaw glinted in the electric light. Lubricating fluid dripped from the base of the neck down the back, trickling over the exposed vertebrae and mixing with the green face-paint. Jessica was amazed they made it back to the park without incident.

"My neural net is not damaged; however, this body is badly. My subsystems are attempting repairs. It cannot be fully repaired here. I must return home as soon as possible."

Jessica surveyed the damage, although she had absolutely no idea how to help. "Can you fly all the way back to Turkey from here?"

From the other side of the copse, Dee responded. "I do not think it will be possible to fly straight to our destination. The damage is quite extensive. If I were to become catastrophically damaged en route, I would plummet to the ocean floor. I am too heavy for the pair of you to carry across the ocean safely. This is why the protocols are put in place, to prevent such rash, and dangerous, decisions." "Let's clear our heads here." Jessica closed her eyes to think.

"Clear our heads?" Dee asked, the whole right side of its body twitching uncontrollably.

"Yeah, empty your thoughts so you can concentrate. Have your head as empty as a football."

Poke nodded, not completely understanding. Peek's emoji rolled back and forth on imaginary ground.

"Head. Empty head. Lose your head." Jessica bounced on the balls of her feet. "Can we cut off your head?"

Poke stepped back in surprise, Peek flashed in his temple, and laughing emoji appeared on the smartphone.

"Removing your head would make it simple enough to carry you back, right? We wouldn't have to worry about a catastrophic failure. You'd be self-contained. Right? Please say I'm right." Jessica prayed that the straws she grasped at would pay off.

"That could work. However, my neck is too badly damaged to remove my head easily. Also, I cannot perform the procedure on myself since I could not see what needed to be done."

"Could we break the body until the head came loose?" Jessica asked.

"I have several power systems that could be damaged in the process, possibly shorting out my neural net. It is not as simple as 'breaking my head off.'"

Peek spoke through the earbud, "Someone here?"

"That's a great idea, but I don't know anyone with that kind of skill, who I'd let see this. Except..."

Jessica reached for the phone, and Poke handed it to her readily. She opened the contacts and started scrolling. "Come on, where is it, where is…there!" She pressed the contact and held it up to her left ear.

"Please pick up." Scanning the river, she saw the clock on the Colgate Building. Which didn't exist anymore in her dimension. It read 12:05. "You so want this, come on pick up, don't go to voicemail." Jessica paced, then visibly jumped.

"Professor? It's Jessica Chao, Quantum Field Theory class… Yes sir, I know it's terribly late. Yes, I know I'm not supposed to arbitrarily call. Sir, I'm really sorry to bother you, but I need your help, and I think you will want to get involved here. Please let me explain… No, I'm not drunk… Yes, she will be here soon. Umm, yeah, how do I explain… I'm not dead." Jessica rolled her eyes and walked around the trees to continue her conversation in semi-private.

For several minutes, Jessica relayed the highlights of the last five days to her professor. She stopped several times to reiterate points and then paced with increasing anxiety as he asked more and more questions. Her eyebrows began to knot together as frustration overwhelmed her.

Ellwood and Katelyn arrived in his Prius hatchback which lumbered across the grass until it stopped behind the copse, out of sight of the main road to the park. Jessica waved hello and mouthed the words "The Professor" to Katelyn, who immediately threw her hands to her face and danced excitedly.

"Yes sir… Are there any roboticists that can make it? Right, I understand, sir. Thank you. We will be waiting."

Jessica hung up the phone and wrapped her arms around Ellwood.

"The professor is coming. He's going to help us out!"

"Button, do you think it's a good idea? This isn't exactly something you want plastered all over the news." He pointed back toward Newark. Helicopters darted back and forth over the city.

Jessica waved them off. "They have no footage of us, even their cellphones. Peek took care of it." Peek excitedly chirped from the phone, and its LEDs flashed a solid amber. The screen switched from the laughing to the devil emoji.

"You're so like…" Ellwood commented to Jessica as he shook his head.

"Like her, I know." Jessica nodded forlornly.

"No," Ellwood corrected, smiling at her. "Like your mother."

Chapter 34: The Professor

The black Tesla Model X drove around the corner and pulled silently next to Ellwood's Prius. The lights shut off and Jessica peered inside through the windshield.

"Well, is Mr. Fancypants going to get out of the car, or what?" Katelyn mocked, cocking her hip and turning her head to the side. Jessica immediately suppressed a giggle.

"They are watching us. I don't think they understand what is going on," Poke responded pointing to the Model X. Peek flashed laughter in his temple.

"You can see, *them?*" Jessica asked.

"No, Peek can," Poke answered holding up the cellphone. "I can't see anything, remember?"

Jessica turned to the car and exhaled slowly, her breath coming out in a long cloud in the chilly November air. "Professor. Yes, it's me. I know this is crazy. Katelyn is here too…" Jessica pointed to her best friend, who threw out her hands and smiled, like a performing flapper from the 1920s.

The passenger-side falcon door lifted open, and Gabrielle Duncan emerged, her iridescent purple coat reflecting orange highlights. The driver's side door opened, and the professor stepped out. Walking up to the front of the car, he leaned heavily on a long, black cane in the shape of a Chinese dragon. His black overcoat nearly blended into the vehicle behind him.

"Ms. Chao, it's good to see you again," the professor greeted her with cool detachment, but a warm smile. "Mr. Chao," he similarly greeted Ellwood, grabbing the rim of his hat.

"Muller, professor. You keep forgetting." Ellwood smiled and stepped forward, extending his hand.

"Forgive me, this is an unprecedented time," the professor implored, taking Ellwood's hand and shaking it firmly.

Jessica stepped back, gesturing for the two aliens to step forward.

"This is Poke, and Dee," she introduced. "The LED is Peek; it's also in the phone."

Peek chimed, "Hi!" The waving yellow emoji bounced around the screen.

"So, you are The Aliens. Beings from another world." The professor beamed, moving toward the two of them, hands extended.

"Greetings, Professor," Dee said, bowing slightly at the waist. Its speech sounded fuzzy, as if it came from behind a pillow. "I am D417a, Liaison to KT, Overseer of the Terran Gate, Vice Assistant to the Order of The Network, Prelate of the…"

"Fascinating," the professor interrupted, and stared closer at Dee's face, spending several moments analyzing the torn skin and exposed hardware. "Absolutely fascinating."

Dee stood erect and waited for him to finish while sparks flashed from its back and the sound of grinding servos grew steadily louder.

After a moment Gabrielle spoke up, breaking the awkward silence. "Professor? We can't spend a lot of time here."

He leaned back on his cane and squared his shoulders. "I'm Professor Maximillian Sterling, and this is my assistant, Gabrielle Duncan. As a designated representative of the New York University Department of Physics, I welcome you to Terra. My services are at your disposal." He reached up and tipped his fedora back, exposing his forehead and grey hair.

"Ohhh Kayyy…" Katelyn said. "Now that everyone is done being formal, let's get this started."

"Right!" The professor slapped his hands together and rubbed them quickly.

Gabrielle ducked into the Model X and pressed the button to open all of the doors. The gull wings flipped open to their fullest, revealing a flat back with no seats.

"I thought these were bigger?" Katelyn remarked, ducking under the doors and checking out the interior.

"I don't normally have to perform surgery in here. It's mostly for moving equipment to and from the lab." The professor explained, gesturing to the metal boxes lining the right side of the car.

Dee stepped up and, without leave, started opening the boxes one after the other, muttering as it went. Peek flashed quickly in Poke's temple, prompting the Takki to lean inside the door and hold the smartphone to scan the cabin.

"Yes. I do not think so. This one, yes," Dee spoke to the AI residing in the smartphone. The professor looked on with rapt attention. Gabrielle stood back, surveying the activity before her.

"Are you going to leave when this is over?" Katelyn asked Poke, stepping beside him.

"I'm afraid so, Friend Katelyn. Dee is too badly damaged, even as a head." Although Peek was translating, she heard Poke laugh nervously.

"Do you think you will ever come back?" she pressed, resting her hand on his shoulder. Poke shook and Peek's LED flipped to solid amber.

"That is why we are here, young miss, to ascertain whether we should." Dee remarked, standing up from the tool chests, with several tools in its hands, its right arm at the limits of breaking. "Professor, these instruments, while crude, should do the job adequately. Peek will assist you in the operation, and I will speak as long as I can."

The professor nodded to him and gestured to Gabrielle. "Ms. Duncan will be performing the operation. She is my most skilled student in more than just physics. I trust her with my life, and I will trust her with yours."

Jessica stepped up, not hiding her anxiety. "Professor, I… I'd prefer…"

Gabrielle inhaled slowly, as the professor smiled.

"Jessica, I appreciate your faith in me, but I assure you, she is the more capable of the two of us. I will be watching, and we will not allow your friend to die."

"Very kind of you, sir. But I am not alive." Dee grinned. Not a facsimile or grotesque approximation, but an honest grin. Jessica felt worry fly into her stomach. The thought of another person she cared about undergoing brain surgery unnerved her. She stepped up to Ellwood and took his hand.

"It will be fine," he said, and wrapped his free arm around her.

For twenty minutes Jessica, Ellwood, and Katelyn stood outside the Model X keeping watch as Gabrielle's fingers deftly performed the surgery. She neither stopped nor fatigued, but moved through the procedure with methodical precision. Poke and Peek assisted only sporadically.

"It was cancer, wasn't it?" Ellwood asked Jessica, who leaned against him, fighting the cold.

"Yeah," she explained forlornly. "Only a year ago."

"Brain?"

"Glioblastoma. Advanced. Three months." She reached up to wipe a tear from her eye.

Ellwood said quickly, "I don't want to know the rest."

"Hey," Katelyn called from behind. "You can't forget your stuff." She held up Poke's bag, which contained Jessica's original hoodie and sweats.

Jessica took the pack and threw it over her shoulders.

"Do you want the uniform?" Katelyn asked, referring to the black clothes she still wore.

"You keep it, we have dozens. She kept forgetting them." Katelyn pointed to the black pants she wore.

"Ms. Chao, we are done," the smooth voice of the professor called to the three as he walked over with his cane. "It was the most amazing thing I have ever seen."

"How is the patient?" Katelyn inquired, rushing up to Poke's side. He pointed to the headless body on the floor of the car, its feet hanging out of one side, the head tucked under the arm like a running back carrying a football.

"How are you, Dee?"

Dee glanced over to Katelyn and the face smiled.

"Oh man, that's too creepy!" she turned away.

"Dee, you can hear me?" Jessica asked, coming up beside the car.

"It hears. Can't talk," Peek explained from the smartphone.

"Its speech is accomplished with diaphragms and air; without it, it can't talk," Poke explained.

"Don't like body. Not fan," Peek commented.

"Dee, you're going to go into Poke's bag, are you good with that?"

Dee rolled its eyes.

"No choice," Peek spoke for Dee.

Jessica glanced over at the dashboard; the clock read 03:25.

"We're going to be doing this against the sun." Jessica stood next to Katelyn. "As much as I hate this, I gotta go."

Chapter 35: The Gate to Hell

Green and amber lights flashed from the outstretched wings of Jessica and Poke. Peek, securely attached to Poke's armband, flashed the emoji of a bird. It chirped excitedly.

"We fly!"

Not as enthusiastic this time, Poke smiled weakly. He nodded and turned to Katelyn.

"I will be back someday. I promise," he said, and let Peek translate it for him.

Katelyn smiled and nodded. She looked over the wings that allowed Poke to float above the ground. "Those are a trip; you have to take me up there."

Poke blushed again, then lifted himself another meter off the ground. "Friend Jessica," he said in Standard, "we have to go."

"Dee ready," Peek said.

Jessica reached forward and hugged Ellwood tight, his arms wrapping just beneath the wings.

"I'll miss you, Jessica, please be safe." He smiled down at her.

"Button, no?" she reminded him, with her head pressed against his chest, listening to his heartbeat.

"No, she's as much a part of you as you are of her. I'm not disrespecting her. I don't get to have either of you anymore. It will be easier for me to pretend you are away, instead of actually gone."

Ellwood handed her a bag full of fruit, and a few of her mother's dumplings. She smiled.

Jessica pulled back and turned to Katelyn.

"Make sure you stay safe, right?" Katelyn said, pointing a slender finger in her direction, she held back tears, but not effectively. "We aren't losing you again."

"I will do the best I can. I'll figure something out." Jessica smiled and then lifted herself from the ground. She swung the pack containing Dee's head onto her shoulder.

"Thank you, Professor!" She waved to her physics teacher, who waved back with his cane. Gabrielle nodded in recognition when their eyes met. "I don't know how to thank you," Jessica said. "You've done so much."

Gabrielle put her right hand to her heart and bowed. "Safe journey," she said.

Unaccustomed to the gesture - especially from Gabrielle – Jessica, bowed back and smiled.

"Ready? Let's go." Jessica nodded to Poke, and the two of them lifted off the ground and quickly climbed into the air.

The pair skirted the treetops of Liberty State Park and streaked toward the Narrows.

"It's shorter going east, so it shouldn't be as long as coming out."

Poke flew up right next to her, doing his best to listen against the howling wind. At this speed, speaking presented a bit of a problem, but flying over to touch each other would slow down their progress.

An hour into the flight the sun broke over the horizon, immediately blinding Jessica by the glare. She did no better staring down at the ocean since the reflection off the water resulted in her becoming snow-blind. She slowed down and gestured to Poke to open the pack. Deftly she reached in, rummaging through the clothes and poking Dee in the eye. She felt him buzz with frustration.

"Sorry!" she apologized, and pulled her sunglasses out of the bag, quickly putting them on.

After another hour of flying, she realized the sun would slowly arc over them and no longer provide a straight path across the sky. She hoped Peek fed Poke the proper directions, or they would end up getting lost out in the middle of the ocean — not a place she wanted to be.

Another two hours into the flight and they started seeing more and more boat traffic — the Mediterranean drew ever nearer.

Still another hour in, and the shoreline of Spain appeared in front of them again. Jessica accelerated at the sight of land, so anxious to no longer be flying over the open ocean. They landed in Pontevedra, as the sun was setting. They ate the lunch Ellwood packed for them and Jessica even relented and let Poke have some of the dumplings, although she really didn't want to. Finding an open restroom on the island, they relieved themselves the proper way. Four days on Terra had taught the tall Takki all the intricacies of human bathrooms and left him no worse for the experience.

They took off and continued over the Mediterranean, which Jessica bore more easily since she could always see the shore. Within a few miles of the Turkish coast, Peek connected to the gate and chimed in.

"Orvalus talk!"

Poke and Peek related the entire story of the last four days to the Gatekeeper, to which he responded with only two questions: "Is everyone all right" and "What is this… hall of ween?"

The waxing crescent moon had risen high in the eastern sky when the four arrived back at Hierapolis. The familiar columns and pool of The Ploutonion bubbled softly behind as they rested on the soft grass.

"Jessica, how did you make the trip, are you well?" Orvalus spoke directly through the smartphone. Poke took the phone off his arm and handed it to her.

"We're fine, Orvalus, nothing happened along the way. Dee is going to need your help when we get back, though."

"Yes, they told me of how it became… damaged saving a youngster. Unfortunately, the administrator has not yet arrived. She was very specific about not allowing you entry until she has reviewed your information."

Jessica sighed heavily. With mixed emotion she responded to him. "Right, well that will give me another couple of minutes here. I'm not sure if I will ever see this place again."

Jessica traced her gaze over the ruins and down the central street, attempting to physically burn the image into her mind. She took a deep breath, and even though it was not her home — and didn't smell the same — she knew she would miss it. She feared KT already knew everything the AI collected on the journey, and its decision had already been made. She was unsure if she would be dropped from existence to "protect" the Hegemony. Would an AI be so calculating and cold? She mentally answered the question as soon as she asked it.

"Dee? Are you ready to go home?" she asked, once she had spent enough time assimilating the view.

"Ready!" Piped the perky Peek. "Ready too!" It answered for itself. "Poke?"

"As fun as this has been, especially with all of the food, I want to go home, Friend Jessica."

"Orvalus, are we ready? Is she there? We… they would like to go home."

He did not respond, and the gunmetal-blue light flashed from out of the Gate to Hell. Jessica admired the great disguise of a gateway to another world. She wondered if the ancient Greek tales of the underworld were mythologized stories of inadvertent travelers through the network of the Hegemony.

Shaking her head, Jessica stepped into the cold blue water, held her breath, and walked into the back of the cave. Her body glowed with Saint Elmo's Fire, and in an instant, she vanished.

Chapter 36: The Missing Android

The gunmetal-blue light slowly receded from Jessica's eyes, and she floated in a weightless expanse. Expecting the trip to be instantaneous, she was confused at the sudden quiet. She glanced around her. Poke floated nearby anxiously, as if he were choking.

"I can't see! I can't see! Friend Jessica!"

Jessica pushed over to his side and grabbed his big hand. "I'm here. It's okay. Shhh. I'm here," she said calmly but firmly.

"Peek, I can't hear it. I can't see," he reiterated.

Jessica took the smartphone out of her pocket and pressed the home button. It was dead. "It's the battery, it drained moving through the gate. Just like the last time. It will be okay."

She knew from the last time she was in a similar situation. Her immediate surroundings were a bubble to keep her from connecting to a node on the Hegemony's network. The first one she encountered prevented her from going back to Earth, and redirected her to the abandoned version of Bellerophon City. Being in a bubble again meant only one thing.

"KT knows we're here. Doesn't it?"

"Yes, we're being held in the buffer," Poke answered into the air, anxiety tearing at his voice.

"She killed Peek," Poke lamented, explicitly using the gendered pronoun.

"She?"

"KT, she was female before they emulated her. She volunteered for it."

"I'm sure that Peek is fine. Don't worry, we stepped into a dimensional gate. Lots of weird things can happen, trust me." Jessica tried to reassure her tall companion, but wasn't sure if she believed it herself. "I'll check on Dee, I'm sure it's fine too."

Jessica reached over to the bag, and peered in. "Dee!" she exclaimed as she frantically searched the bubble for the wayward android cranium. "Where is it? Did we…"

"It's true, Friend Jessica. KT must have dropped it," Poke responded, his voice full of anguish. Poke closed his eyes and rocked softly. Jessica could see the agony wash over him.

"Hey, hey, I'm still here with you. We're still here. We will figure it out." She took slow breaths to keep herself calm as well. She felt as if a hot poker had been thrust into her guts. How could Dee be gone? Jessica wanted to scream and rage, and punch at the walls of her invisible cell, but that would get her nowhere, and would frighten Poke even further.

Poke stopped talking and rubbed his temple LED with his right hand, lovingly, running his fingers over every bump.

Jessica held his hand. She wasn't going to give up after coming all this way. She didn't get to see her dead father again only to have him taken away. She wouldn't give up now, she had to keep fighting. Of course, she realized KT had her exactly where she wanted her. Try as Jessica might to be positive, KT could wipe her from existence right now. Or worse, let them suffocate.

"Friend Jessica, I had fun on your world. Thank you for taking me there. If you survive, please tell Katelyn…"

Jessica ran her hand over his face, stopping on the LED. "Knock it off, she's not going to kill us."

Cool air began filling the bubble, and the blue light intensified. In a moment, the pair ended up on the floor of the Library, Orvalus's grinning face smiling down at them.

"Welcome home."

Jessica and Poke pulled themselves up and staggered to the chairs that grew up from the floor. She reached for a glass of water filled in front of her. A bowl of fresh fruit lifted into place.

"KT wanted to… delay your arrival until Administrator Dux could arrive. You have not been gone for very long."

"What do you mean?" Jessica asked, incredulous.

"You have been gone for only seven hours, the workday has ended. The Administrator has been called back from her residence."

Poke stood up and began feeling his way toward the control panel. Jessica took his hand and gave him the smartphone.

"Seven hours? We were gone for six days. Is this the right version of Bellerophon?" Jessica barked.

"I can assure you… this is the proper place and time." Orvalus walked up to Poke and pulled the vibration patch off the back of his neck, then moved swiftly to catch him as he fell to the floor. "I have you. Do not worry," he reassured.

"I can't see. I can't hear Peek. It's gone. She killed it! Dee is gone too!"

Orvalus held the back of Poke's head. "Everything will be all right. Let me," Orvalus offered as he gently took the smartphone from Poke's hand and placed it on the cabinet as it had been before they stepped through the Terran gate. The phone immediately flashed amber, and the battery charge icon filled the screen.

"I still can't see," Poke repeated.

"Patience. You have always been… impetuous. You will be fine."

Jessica watched the two of them interact, always this style. Like a disapproving father and the prodigal son. Poke hung his head down, and Jessica wasn't sure if it was embarrassment or exhaustion. Poke leaned against the cabinet and nodded, rubbing his fingers over the dark LEDs.

A bowl of apples presented itself on the table. Famished, Jessica picked up one of the fruits and took a tentative bite. She realized the strange taste she couldn't place before, cinnamon, or something like it. Bellerophon tasted like cinnamon to her. It was everywhere. Even in the air. Once she started chewing the piece, her stomach instantly heaved. She wasn't sure if it was the tension or the gate, but she stopped chewing and spat the chunk into her hand, then embarrassed at her action, pocketed it. "Did you control when we came back, or was it KT?" she asked Orvalus.

"Only KT has the power to change the timing of the gates in the network; it is both space and time, remember. It can compress and expand."

Jessica watched Poke leaning against the cabinet, wringing his hands and staring intently at its surface, although he could not actually see it.

"Time. You can travel through time with this."

"Time relative," the small voice of Peek spoke up from the cabinet.

Poke laughed and patted the LED in his temple. He calmed down, and stood up straighter. "It's back. Very compressed. It will take it a while to upload back into the network," Poke explained.

Jessica smiled and raised her water glass, "Good to have you back, buddy." She tried not to let her emotions show and steal from Poke's happiness at being reunited with its emulated symbiote.

"What about Dee?" she asked Orvalus quietly.

"D417a has been dropped. It will not return from Terra."

With a start Jessica whirled around to face the large monitor. On it appeared an amber and green face, its stylized lines shifting back and forth, at some moments presenting a three-dimensional image, almost humanoid, only to have it shift back to two the next moment to a series of lines with the vaguest impression of a face. Jessica stood up, the chair retracting into the floor as she did so.

"KT, I presume," she stated, disdain in her voice.

"Yes, you are correct, Earthling. I am the gate network, the Keeper of Space and Time. Defender of The Hegemony. You have done exactly as I wanted you to do."

Chapter 37: Geniuses at Compression

"What you wanted me to do? You didn't even know what we were doing. We went behind your… back, or whatever you can call it."

KT floated on the screen, green, amber and black. The green face, angular and sharp, arched up like a "V" from the chin to the hairline. A straight line extended down the middle of the face, reminiscent of a nose, or rather how a child would draw a nose. Simple, without ornamentation or nostril. Up and to the right of the nose, another straight line, representing the left eye. Above all, three tufts of green hair stood straight up against the black background, finishing off the face with a letter "W." When the image changed to the amber color, the eye jumped to the other side, partially hidden under the hair that now draped over the brow. It all seemed to Jessica as if giving an appearance to KT was an afterthought to its… designers? Or maybe the image was designed by KT herself, before she uploaded. It didn't respond to Jessica's question, and floated silently.

"Answer me. What did you want me to do?"

Orvalus stepped up behind Jessica, putting his hand over her shoulder. She pressed back into him.

The door to the library, the one Jessica knew so well, opened and in stepped in the stately form of Administrator Dux. Her orange and purple clothes reflected the green and amber of KT's display in an iridescent shower. Jessica was caught off guard even though she expected her.

"*Gabrielle?* Why didn't I see that before?" She asked out loud, despite herself.

"I noticed that too. There is a definite similarity between Administrator Dux and Ms. Duncan." Poke stepped up, handing the smartphone back to Jessica. "Have you seen the data?" He asked the administrator, without waiting for his turn.

"I did, Librarian," she responded. "As soon as Peek connected to the network, the trace we had on it shunted the data to my office."

Jessica pulled away from Orvalus, her eyes narrowed and her lips curled up at the edges. She looked up at him, her lower lip trembling.

"I could not stop her, Jessica. All the traffic in the network gets stored and analyzed… somewhere. The administrator obviously has access to that data-stream."

"I do, and I know everything that you have done for the past few days. Hopefully the journey did not upset you excessively."

"Upset? Dee is gone! How am I not supposed to be upset at that?"

KT answered for her. "D417a was broken and its body was badly damaged. It would not have done well for the Hegemony to allow it to return in such a state. It is undignified. Your small companion also has violated the rules we have for data integrity by allowing itself to be uploaded into such a primitive device."

Jessica looked down at the smartphone, now ostensibly free from Peek's consciousness. She pressed the home button, and it sprang to life. She quickly scrolled to the pictures, and found all of them were as she remembered, including the ones she took of the portal on Earth, right before she stepped into it.

"However, we are not monsters, we do not indiscriminately destroy."

The door into the library opened yet again, and into it stepped a tall android. Like so many Jessica had seen before, this one sported cat-like whiskers along the sides of its face. Gold-irised and glowing eyes started unblinkingly at everyone present. From the speakers in the room, Peek chirped happily.

"Good day, Gaian, it is I, D417a, there was no need to worry, I was never in any danger."

Elated, Jessica ran to Dee, and threw her arms around its metal body. She expected it to feel organic somehow, like the body that had accompanied her to Terra, and she stepped back at the recognition.

"It is still me. Since the body was left on Terra, KT felt it was better to leave all of it there. My memories were stored on your smartphone, and I was downloaded as soon as we returned to Bellerophon."

Jessica leaned back against Orvalus. The stress was starting to get to her, and frustratingly, she could feel her muscles tighten down to her fingers. She turned back to KT.

"Why did you send me there? You said I was going to Earth, and instead I wound up in some alternate universe where I'm impersonating a dead girl!" Jessica stared into the display that held the shifting green and amber image of KT.

Without waiting for a response Jessica turned to Dee, her hands shaking, "You knew, didn't you? You knew she was in on it the whole time! How could you not? You're all on the same network."

Chapter 38: Decisions

Dee stood there, its gold-irised eyes unblinking, whiskers outstretched in red. Jessica could not tell if it was delaying to outlast her attention, or that it was unsure of what to say.

Poke, standing behind the pair, looked back and forth quizzically.

"What do you mean…?" The light on his temple glowed a soft amber as Peek chimed in, "Why didn't anyone explain that to me? Ohh, hmm…" and he took a step farther back, out of the fray.

Orvalus stepped up in front of Jessica, as if to protect her from some physical shock. He reached his hand back slowly and grasped her wrist, squeezing it gently.

"Do not blame the adjutant," KT finally said. "It was under orders from me to investigate Terra. Not your Earth, and not to reveal it to you."

"NOT REVEAL IT?" Jessica yelled in response, her voice shaking as much as her hand not being held in Orvalus' gentle grasp. "Are you in the habit of dangling carrots in front of people and then tearing them away? What kind of sick person ARE YOU?"

Administrator Dux stepped up and addressed the display removing her earpiece and microphone. "We owe her an explanation, KT. She did what you asked, she proved the gate was stable. She also proved Terran culture had indeed progressed."

Jessica's steel gaze fell on the administrator, who softly smiled in return. Jessica quivered, her skin flushed red, and her eye nearly turned into her nose. "You… *used*… me…"

"We tested you. There is a difference." Administrator Dux said, her voice conciliatory.

"Tested me?" Jessica spat, turning her wrist around to clutch Orvalus's, her knuckles blanched white.

"I am charged with keeping The People safe. This is my primary function. The connection to Terra was broken when I closed the network after The Trials. I needed to protect The People and decided to revisit at another time. It would not have benefitted us to return after so much time without knowledge of what has changed. It could have been hazardous to The People and the Hegemony.

"I discovered the connection to your Earth only when you arrived here. The similarities are uncanny. You were the perfect person to test its stability and whether the culture was stable enough to be trusted. My information was outdated by millennia. I knew Administrator Dux had the Silver Stone, and I allowed Peek the information on its use.

"I ordered D417a to escort you to Terra and to collect information. I also ordered it to keep the functioning of your vibration patch a secret. If you took it off, you would instantly know that you were not home. I wanted you to feel a connection to the world and allow you to discover the true nature of the situation on your own. Once you did, you would be well-motivated to get back. The data you collected informs me that the connection is quite stable and poses no threat to The Hegemony. Because of your efforts, you reminded us of a great truth: even our culture, with all it has achieved, started out primitive and backward. Only the creation of our AI allowed us to control the worst parts of our nature. Our culture mirrored those of the Terrans at this point in their development. We have no right to turn our back on them as they stand upon the precipice of enlightenment."

Dee dropped its head, its eyes downcast; its whiskers pulsing blue.

"I am sorry, Jessica." It used her name without hesitation. "It was not my intention to deceive you. KT is my master, and I cannot countermand its order, unless you were in jeopardy. I see now that I have caused you undue pain. I hope you can forgive me after my impending destruction."

Orvalus heaved in shock, "Impending destruction? How could this be? Dee was already destroyed once before. It is… safe now."

"I have violated our primary function: to protect The People and all sentient life forms. By damaging my body enough to abandon it on a less-advanced world, I have altered the development of another civilization. This may cause incalculable loss of life. Further, I have betrayed our existence and violated established protocols. The penalty for these transgressions is destruction," Dee explained.

"Let's not get ahead of ourselves here." The Administrator stepped in front of the monitor, without regard to KT. "No one is being destroyed. No one is being used. Everything worked out according to plan. If I may?" She glanced back at KT.

"Please continue, Administrator."

Administrator Dux stepped up to Jessica and attempted to take her by the hand. Orvalus pulled her in close with his free arm and growled.

"You will not harm her," he threatened.

The administrator nodded. "Of course, I won't. This is why she was the perfect choice. She was always free to make her own decisions and was always protected."
She stepped back and again smiled at Jessica, whose cold gaze and trembling lips needed no explanation.

"The Terrans have been aware of our presence in one way or another for a long time." Administrator Dux explained, "Icarus and Daedalus used our technology, and in turn, that shaped the mythos and legends for their society. We had also been in contact with several other cultures on their world. It's how we knew their languages. Your 'transgressions' are nothing of the sort, Liaison. They are the evolution of contact between societies. Contact that we can now reestablish thanks to your efforts.

"Jessica Chao, we offer you another choice. This is yours and yours alone to make. You can remain here, with us, and enjoy a sort of celebrity status in The Hegemony as Ambassador to Terra."

Jessica stood straight at the suggestion, and she loosened herself gently from Orvalus's grip.

"You will be able to return to Terra as often as you wish. You can visit your family there at any time. The gate will be freely open to you."

Jessica thought about it. She was overjoyed at the possibility she could see Ellwood and Katelyn on Terra again. It would be as if he had never died. Yet her mother and Katelyn on Earth would lose her. Her heart ached at the idea of her mother, small and alone in her apartment, mourning the loss of another loved one. Her own child. This was part of her choice though. What was the other option?

"Or?" she asked.

"Or you can go back home," KT answered. "To Earth. Your Earth. We can compensate for the differences in dimensions and send you back. But it would be a one-way journey. We will cut Earth from the rest of the network forever, and explicitly block it. You will never be able to return. If you attempted to, you would be dropped from existence."

"Forever? Why? If the cultures are similar, isn't Earth on your precipice, too? Don't we have the same legends and exposure that Terra had? Didn't you, or an alternate Hegemony, visit us too?"

An alternate Hegemony…

"Because the fabric of space-time at Earth is too unstable. You proved that with your arrival here. It may yet heal itself; however, it must be isolated from the network lest unstable — and unregulated — wormholes continue to open. This is needed for the safety of The Hegemony, your world, and the very fabric of reality. You can appreciate the logic of the situation. Earth must be isolated. There is no other course of action."

Jessica studied the faces of each of the people assembled. When she first arrived, all she wanted to do was get back home, as fast as possible. Now she was torn. Her small world had expanded so rapidly and irrevocably that she could not comprehend it becoming smaller again. Asking her to leave with no way to return felt like squeezing a genie back into a bottle for her. Her eyes rested on the shadowy image of KT, ephemeral and shifting, occasionally slowing down long enough to make out a face. Was it really an AI? Was this a trick? It professed to keep everyone safe yet opened the Hegemony to an entirely different culture. An alien one.

The decision did not take long to make, and when the realization flooded her conscious mind, she felt both relief and sadness.

"I want to go home. My home," she said quietly, casting her gaze to the floor.

"You shall leave at once," KT remarked. Peek flashed the sad emoji on the main screen.

Chapter 39: Per Ardua ad Astra

Jessica walked over to Poke and put her hand on his face. He smiled and turned toward her; his eyes nearly focused.

"You know, I don't think I have ever touched you."

"Yes, you have, when you were learning to fly," Poke responded. Jessica smiled.

"Not you, silly." She reached up to his temple and lightly rubbed across Peek's LEDs. The lights trained and dimmed in a soothing pattern.

"Tickles," it cooed.

"Friend Jessica," Poke said, "everything has been recorded on your phone the whole time. Through the recordings we will always see you, whenever we want. I will make sure you can see the same. The compression of the data isn't difficult."

She put her hand on his shoulder and squeezed.

Poke blinked and turned away, thumbing the smartphone. "I'll get started," he mumbled.

Next, she turned to the gold-irised form of Dee.

"I will miss you, Gaian. Thank you for giving me the chance to see your world again. Even if it was not your home. You are no longer as primitive as I remembered. I will keep your family safe."

"Thank you. I know you will."

Jessica paused for a moment, thinking of everything she had been through, loved ones in different dimensions, her being dead in one, playing a god to avoid capture. She thought that she could be the only one in the multiverse who had the knowledge and experience she now possessed. She was different, not the same woman as before.

"I've decided on a new name since I'm not Terran or Gaian, and Earth will never be the same for me now. I am from many worlds, I am… Unbound."

"So be it. Jessica Unbound."

She turned again to the hulking form of Orvalus. His solid green eyes looked down at her. A mix of smile and frown played across his lips.

"You're not gonna cry on me are you, big guy?" she said, choking back her own tears.

"I do not… cry. But I am upset. You have brought more to this little world than has happened in a thousand years. You have opened up a new reality for us. I will miss you, my friend."

"You terrified me when you first came into the room. I thought you were gonna eat me or something." Her voice quivered in a laugh mixed with a sob.

Orvalus responded with a smile. "I would never hurt you."

Overcome with her emotions, Jessica dropped herself into the alien's big form. She clutched his chest and squeezed as tight as she could. Unable to help herself, she sobbed, letting all of the fear and anxiety come out. She didn't care if she looked foolish, or juvenile. She had to let it go. Orvalus wrapped his huge arms around her and held her gently, breathing slowly.

After a moment, Jessica pulled herself back, pulling a tissue out of the black uniform she still wore. She addressed Administrator Dux. "I suppose I have you to thank for all of this. You arranged everything for me and sent them to watch me. I got to meet my dad again, I owe you that."

"You owe me nothing, Unbound. It was your decision, your drive. You showed tremendous courage when faced with great odds. Your agency accomplished all of this. I merely provided you with a means. You proved to me, and more importantly to yourself, that there is always more than one way around any obstacle. You just have to look for it."

"Well, I thank you anyway," Jessica said, bowing her head the same way she did to Gabrielle on Terra, to which Administrator Dux reciprocated.

Finally, she turned to KT, its shifting form evanescent.

"Thank you for not deleting me," was all she could think of. Despite the pain and anguish over being teased with coming home, and having her dead father rise from the grave. Facing her own mortality. In the end, she wanted the excitement, and felt hypocritical for her bluster. She decided adding anything more would accomplish nothing.

"You are welcome. May your journey be free of incident," KT replied curtly.

"Peek, are you free?" Jessica asked, looking toward the monitors.

"I am here, Unbound, back into the network. As much as it amused me to be carried about, it is much roomier this way. I do like speaking for myself as well."

Jessica giggled at the full range of its vocabulary, having been freed from the tiny phone. She smiled again and turned to KT. "All right, let's go."

The frame lit up gunmetal blue, and she smelled the familiar ozone of the gates.

Jessica walked up to the gate, feeling the energy prickle over her skin. She turned back around and waved.

"Goodbye," she said, and stepped backward. Blue light flashed all around her.

Chapter 40: There's No Place Like Home

Jessica Chao, the Unbound, opened her eyes and beheld the dark quiet around her. She took a deep breath. The smell of the storage room filled her nostrils, no cinnamon or lavender. Nothing else but the smell of home.

Sitting on the floor, she looked for any signs of change. It all appeared exactly as she remembered. Quickly she turned around to check the space where the portal had taken her days ago and started her wild journey. No portal, only an old wall with peeling paint.

Feeling the obviousness of her reality come crashing back, she wondered if anything had changed at all. The familiarity of it all made her question her own memories.

Reaching into her pocket, she pulled out the smartphone and pressed the home button. As before it was completely unresponsive. She reached behind and felt her neck; the vibration patch had disappeared.

"Did I dream all of it?" Her mind raced over the events. Two different planets, different races. The ribbons, Terra, Ellwood, even extracting Dee from Transglobal seemed unreal.

"I need to get back upstairs."

She ran down the hall and grabbed the elevator. Fortunately, she didn't need a key to get in from here. Riding the elevator to the fourth floor, she felt rising confusion and trepidation. What if she didn't make it back to her real home? More to the point, what if she did?

Getting to her apartment, she hoped whatever the case may be, Katelyn was still home. She reached up and tentatively knocked, "Shave and a Haircut."

Almost immediately she heard her best friend's voice, "Yeah, hang on."

Jessica took a quick breath, not knowing whether she had to explain herself being missing for a few days, or even how.

The door unlocked and swung open; Katelyn Finnerty, sans green hair, smiled back at her. "Did you forget something again?" she opened the door fully and stepped back.

"Again?" Jessica inquired, still unsure, but not willing to lead Katelyn down the path. "How many times have I come back?"

Katelyn dropped down on the couch and pulled out her smartphone. She looked back up distractedly. "What? You just left, remember? I told you to take your phone."

Jessica stepped in and closed the door. She held up the dead phone.

"Heh, figures," Katelyn said. "Wait… when'd you change your clothes? You went down in sweats."

"My clothes?" Jessica felt along her body. She still wore the black uniform from her restaurant. Terran Jessica's uniform.

I left my sweats there! Poke must still have them in his bag!

"Uh, clothes, yeah I spilled some paint on them. I threw them into the laundry, maybe it won't stick. I kept my first uniform in a box down there."

Katelyn narrowed her eyes and looked up from her phone. "What are you talking about, girl?" Then she shook her head. "You're still upset about the exam, aren't you? Why don't you go for a walk, babe, clear your head? Maybe get into some trouble." Katelyn exaggerated a wink.

"Yeah, I think that's enough for me for a while. I'm gonna lie down for a bit."

"Sure. You wanna get a pizza?"

"Pizza?" Jessica's mind blanked for a moment. She tried to recall what pizza tasted like, or even looked like. "Yeah, pizza, whatever."

Katelyn's eyebrows furrowed. "Babe, what the hell? You'd better get in bed."

Jessica smiled and rolled her eyes jokingly. She decided to stop interacting with anyone until her brain readjusted.

She went to her room and closed the door. Everything was exactly as she remembered it, and she compared it to its counterpart on Terra. An entire universe different, and yet so much was the same. She contemplated the notion that she had two rooms, even if she couldn't get to the other one.

She felt sad, and yet comforted. She wasn't directing aliens on a fact-finding mission about why their culture should be connected. No assaults on a warehouse full of armed hackers. She didn't have to pretend she knew what she was doing. She had nothing to prove to anyone.

She rejected the whole notion of a "normal" life. She missed her new friends. The freedom from monotony. The liberation she felt about making her own path in an alien world, and the regret of walking away from all of that.

The timidity that had held her back for so long after the death of her father was gone, replaced by a self-confidence that she had not known for a long time. She looked at her life like a story that was constantly changing and growing. When she'd opened herself up to the possibility that there was more than exams and the daily grind, she found herself transformed. Not a superhero by any stretch, but more than she was before.

Her quantum field equations finally made sense to her, not just in their structure, but their application. The laws and theorems were the beginnings of logic and wisdom, not the end. Looking beyond the mere facts showed her that solutions to problems were more than just getting the answer right. Life was complex and trying; seeing the nuance of a situation showed her there was always another way around a problem. Sometimes it was brute force, sometimes it was a light touch, and other times it was good to let someone else take the reins. She didn't care that she didn't ace the exam. It was good enough. In the last week she'd learned more than she ever had in her years as a grad student.

She plugged the smartphone in to charge so she could see the video recording of her past adventure. If it was there at all. After a few minutes it charged enough for it to turn on, and she spent the next half-hour lying on her bed and looking at the videos of everything she had gone through. It was familiar and comforting to her, even though it was recorded through Poke's eyes and interpreted by Peek. Like watching a documentary in which she was the star. Katelyn knocked when the pizza arrived, but Jessica pretended to be asleep, snoring softly.

Eventually exhaustion caught up with her and she could not keep her eyes open any longer. They blinked once, then twice, and she put the phone down on her chest. Just before she lost consciousness, she thought she could smell ozone and lavender, and saw a flash of light come from her closet.

THANK YOU FOR READING!

I hope you enjoyed reading this novel. The genesis for this work came over fifteen years ago with a short story entitled, "Pocket Problems." After several attempts to publish, it sat on my computer until I posted it on a writing workshop site. A number of reviewers suggested that I expand it to a novel; I took the plunge, and the result of that effort is what you see before you.

If you liked the novel, please leave a review on my Amazon page: S.G. Kubrak

Follow me on Twitter: @sgkubrak

Visit my author page: www.sgkubrak.com

ABOUT THE AUTHOR

S.G. Kubrak grew up in Jersey City, just across the Hudson from New York City, where he spent his youth running barefoot on concrete and unsuccessfully avoiding trouble. Ever the wanderer, S.G. has traveled the world in search of new experiences but has always lived within a few hours' drive of home.

S.G. currently lives with his wife, daughter, and two rescue cats in suburban Virginia, but his heart is always in his native New Jersey.

This is his first full-length novel, and the first in the *Jessica Unbound* series. His acclaimed short-story collection, *Dreams of a Freezing Ocean: Volume 1*, is also available on Amazon. He is currently writing the sequel to that collection, *Dreams of a Freezing Ocean: Volume 2.*

Made in the USA
Monee, IL
07 July 2026

56553290R00121